It's Sho

As showtime drew near o[...] dashed up to them, looking [...] seen the Browning's electrician?" she asked. "We're having trouble with the lights, and we can't find him."

"We haven't seen him," Phil replied. "But I've done all the lighting in the Bayport High productions for the last three years. I could probably fill in if you want me to."

"The union will kill me if they find out," Ms. Greenberg said, "but we can't wait any longer. Go for it, Phil."

Phil nodded and headed up the spiral stairs leading to the big catwalks overhead.

"Don't worry," Frank said. "Phil's a wizard with electronics."

"He'd better be," Ms. Greenberg replied.

The Hardys and their girlfriends looked up to where Phil was working on the lighting. Suddenly Phil lurched over the edge of the catwalk and slipped toward the stage below.

The Hardy Boys
Mystery Stories

Available from ALADDIN Paperbacks

THE **HARDY BOYS**®

#185
WRECK AND ROLL

FRANKLIN W. DIXON

Aladdin Paperbacks
New York London Toronto Sydney

This book is a work of fiction. Any references to historical events,
real people, or real locales are used fictitiously. Other names, characters, places,
and incidents are the product of the author's imagination,
and any resemblance to actual events or locales or persons, living or dead,
is entirely coincidental.

First Aladdin Paperbacks edition June 2004
Copyright © 2004 by Simon & Schuster, Inc.

ALADDIN PAPERBACKS
An imprint of Simon & Schuster
Children's Publishing Division
1230 Avenue of the Americas
New York, NY 10020

The text of this book was set in New Caledonia.

Printed in the United States of America
2 4 6 8 10 9 7 5 3 1

THE HARDY BOYS MYSTERY STORIES is a trademark of Simon & Schuster, Inc.

THE HARDY BOYS and colophon are registered trademarks of Simon & Schuster, Inc.

Library of Congress Control Number 2003112436

ISBN 0-689-86736-0

Contents

1 Band in Bayport

"Grab your dancing shoes and prepare to party!" Phil Cohen announced as he walked into the living room in Joe and Frank Hardy's home. Phil slicked back his dark hair and adjusted the collar of his shirt.

Frank, Joe, and their girlfriends—Callie Shaw and Iola Morton—all laughed. Phil was known for his genius with electronics and his keen intellect, *not* for being cool. Tonight, though, he was dressed to the nines and looked ready to star in a music video.

Phil raised an eyebrow at his friends. "What?" he asked. "Is my shirt hanging out or something?"

"Nope," Frank said. "We're just not used to you being a fashion plate."

"And I think you've forgotten your pocket protector," Joe joked.

"It's keeping my slide rule company at home," Phil replied, chuckling. "Are you all ready to go? The show starts in less than half an hour."

"Are we dressed right for this gig?" Callie Shaw asked. Frank's pretty, blond girlfriend smoothed the creases in her sleek blue skirt and satin top.

"I look like I belong in the Stone Age," Iola Morton agreed. She checked her own casual outfit and frowned. She and Callie looked great, but for the first time ever they weren't nearly as well-dressed as Phil.

Joe Hardy laughed. "What does that make Frank and me?" he asked. "Cave men?" He hitched up his jeans, pulled down his black T-shirt, and ran one hand through his unruly blond hair. "Maybe I should have gotten a new do for tonight's festivities."

"We're just going to a concert," Frank said, "not putting on a fashion show." He put his arm around Callie. "You girls look super. You'll be the envy of every girl there."

"Thanks," Callie said. She took a moment to admire her boyfriend's lean, muscular frame, dark hair, and flashing brown eyes. "You're looking pretty super yourself."

Phil checked his watch. "Well, we'll all be looking *late* if we don't get a move on." He opened the Hardys' front door and waved his friends forward. "My chariot awaits. Let's hit the road."

"Well-dressed *and* impatient," Joe said, his blue

2

eyes twinkling. "We're seeing a whole new side of the Philmeister."

"Less talk, more hustle," Phil said, pretending to kick Joe's rear end.

Phil and the others hustled toward his aging green Toyota, which was sitting by the curb.

"Did you buy a bumper-sticker factory?" Frank asked. Bright, adhesive ads covered nearly every available surface of Phil's rusting car.

Callie scanned the names on the stickers. "I didn't know you were such a fan of local music," she said.

A mischievous grin drew over Iola's face. "Phil's not into *all* local music," she observed. "The Vette Smash stickers outnumber the rest, ten to one."

"Hop in," Phil said, holding the car door open. "I'll give you the rundown once we get rolling."

The other teens piled into the car as Phil slid behind the wheel. He pulled the Toyota away from the Hardys' house and onto the main road leading to downtown Bayport.

"Too bad Chet couldn't come with us," Callie said.

"He's helping our grandparents out on the farm this week," Iola said. "The school's even giving him credit for it."

"It's nice that you Mortons are keeping touch with your roots," Frank said.

Iola nodded. "That farm's been in our family for generations. Even though we live in the city now, it's nice to go back for vacations and stuff."

"Maybe Joe and I can tag along sometime," Frank suggested.

"That'd be fun," Iola agreed.

"So, Phil," Joe said, "what's the deal between you and Vette Smash? Are they paying you to advertise or what?"

"I think the stickers are all that's holding this old heap together," Frank said. "Auto-body work has never been Phil's strong suit."

"Very funny, you guys," Phil said. "Vette Smash is a great band. Tonight's concert will make believers out of all of you."

"I caught a Vette Smash tune on the Bayport High station earlier today," Iola said. "They've been getting a lot of airplay on WBPT, too."

"They're a hot act," Callie agreed. "The Bayport High pep squad is planning to use their music for a couple of numbers this season. Everybody who's anybody is listening to them now."

"Being 'in' has never been Phil's gig, though," Frank said. "I sense something more going on here. Right, Phil?"

Phil turned the car onto Racine Street, heading north toward the harbor. "No need to make a mystery out of it," he said. "I met one of the band's members at an acoustic guitar seminar, and we hit it off."

"And this member's name would be . . . ?" Iola asked. She arched one dark eyebrow at her friend.

4

"Julie Steele," Phil replied, "but in the band she's known as Chrome Jewel."

"Aha!" Iola and Callie chimed simultaneously.

"Hey, it's no big deal," Phil said, smiling sheepishly. "We've just gone out a couple of times. . . ."

"That puts this case to rest," Joe said, leaning back in his seat. "Any guy would support his new girlfriend's band."

Phil turned slightly red. "Busted."

"Nothing slips past these guys," Iola said, laughing.

"Or their nosy girlfriends," Frank added with a smile.

"Okay," Phil said. "But even if I wasn't going out with Jewel, Vette Smash would still be a great band."

"We'll be the judge of that—after the concert," Joe said. "Where are we seeing them?"

"The old Browning Theater," Phil replied. "Two nights only, two shows a night. The band's got a pretty hectic schedule this week—a lot of promos and stuff. I'm helping out wherever I can."

"And building up the audience by bringing all your friends," Callie noted.

"We don't count as members of the audience," Phil said. "We've got backstage passes."

"So tell us about Julie," Frank said.

"She plays bass and sings," Phil said. "She does some song writing, too, and . . . hey!"

A pickup truck suddenly swerved at them out of the opposite lane. Phil pulled the Toyota toward the side of the road, barely avoiding a car parked by the curb.

"Vette Smash stinks!" called a guy from the truck. He lobbed a soda bottle at the Toyota. Phil swerved left, and the bottle crashed to the street beside them.

The guys in the truck laughed and roared down the road.

"Those rats!" Joe fumed as the pickup drove off. "Go after them, Phil!" He leaned over the front seat to urge Phil forward.

"Take it easy, Joe," Frank said, putting a hand on his brother's shoulder. "Those guys aren't worth getting worked up about. The police patrol this area pretty heavily. If we go after them, we'll probably wind up caught in a car chase with those jerks."

"Frank's right," Callie said.

Joe sat back down. "Yeah, okay," he said. "But letting them get away with lobbing bottles really burns me up."

"They haven't gotten away with it," Iola said. "Look."

As she spoke, a police car pulled out of a side street in front of Phil's Toyota. The cruiser's lights flashed on, and it quickly gained speed. Moments later, the patrol car had pulled the pickup over to the side of the road.

Phil slowly cruised by the police. The Hardys and their friends tried not to grin too much as they passed the bottle tossers.

"That truck has almost as many Green Machine bumper stickers as you have Vette Smash stickers," Joe noted.

"Isn't Green Machine another local band?" Iola asked.

"Yeah," Phil replied. "They have this big rivalry with Vette Smash. I'm not surprised that their fans would throw bottles at us. A lot of Green Machine's audience are real jerks."

"I didn't know being a fan of local music could be so dangerous," Callie said.

"The rivalries get pretty intense sometimes," Phil said. He pulled off the main drag and drove past the Browning Theater.

"Looks like finding a parking space will be pretty intense, too," Frank said. The street in front of the auditorium was jammed with parked cars—unusual for the old building.

The Browning was built in the 1920s as a movie palace. It had been remodeled several times before being turned into a second-run and revival movie house. A popular destination with Bayport movie-goers, the Browning occasionally hosted live music as well.

"A crowd like this ought to help keep the Browning alive," Joe said. "You might find parking closer to the river. There ought to be some spots a couple of blocks down."

"Good idea," Phil said. "Let's drive by the back

first, though, and see if there's something there. We'll be using the stage entrance, anyway."

"Ah," Iola said with a sigh, "the perks of being with the band." They all laughed.

Unfortunately the perks that night *didn't* include a reserved parking spot in the back. The alleys behind the theater were just as crowded as the street in front. Finding nothing, Phil took Joe's suggestion and headed toward the river. They found a parking spot five blocks away and hiked back toward the Browning. The evening was pleasantly cool and none of them minded the walk.

In front of the Browning, a crowd of fans milled around, jostling one another as they pushed through the theater doors. Phil led the Hardys and their girlfriends past the mob and into an alley leading to the back of the old building. As they rounded the alley corner, though, he slapped his head.

"I left the passes in the car!" he said, angry with himself. "You all go hang out by the back door. I'll run back and get them." He turned and hustled away into the darkness.

"I guess following a band has made Phil forgetful as well," Iola said with a smile.

"That's okay," Callie said. "Geniuses like him are pretty much expected to be absentminded."

The four friends continued around the corner to the Browning's back entrance. A long service alleyway ran behind the building, connecting the businesses surrounding the old theater to the side streets on the east and west. Smaller alleys, like the ones the teens had come down, connected the main streets on the north and south sides to the service alley.

"It's like a maze back here," Joe noted.

The stage entrance of the Browning was facing a dead-end alley between two large buildings. A big Dumpster stood near the serviceway, and the scent of stale garbage filled the air. At the far end of the alley, a single lightbulb burned over an old wooden door marked STAGE DOOR.

"So much for the glamour of stardom," Frank said, wrinkling his nose.

Callie shrugged. "I guess everybody's got to work their way up," she said.

A big security guard in a red Vette Smash shirt stood near the door. He folded his arms across his chest and glowered as the Hardys and their girl-friends approached.

"Go around front," the guard said. "You can't come in this way." The ID hanging on a thin chain around his neck identified him as Geo Kaspar.

"We're just waiting for our friend," Joe said. "He left our passes in the car and had to go back to get them."

Kaspar scoffed. "I've heard that one before. I've heard them *all* before. This is a secured area. Move on out of here before I do it for you."

"Cool down," Frank said. "Our friend will be back in a minute or two."

"Are you guys deaf or just stupid?" Kaspar asked. His deep voice echoed menacingly in the alleyway. "No one's allowed back here except the band and their associates. So, vamoose!"

"Maybe *you're* the one who's deaf," Joe snapped. "We said we've *got* passes, and they'll be here in a minute or two. What's your hurry?"

Kaspar rolled up the short sleeves of his shirt, exposing his bulging shoulders and muscular arms. He cracked his knuckles and stepped menacingly toward Joe. "I warned you," he said, "but you just wouldn't listen. . . ."

2 The Bouncer Bounce

"Take it easy," Frank said. He stepped between the bouncer and Joe, trying to head off a fight.

Kaspar put his fist down and shoved Frank aside. Frank's back hit the alley's brick wall, forcing his breath out.

Kaspar tried to grab Joe, but the younger Hardy ducked under the big man's arms. Joe stuck out his foot as Kaspar lumbered past. The bouncer tripped, stopping himself inches before his face hit the wall. He turned, rage burning in his eyes.

"Calm down," Frank said, stepping forward again. "There's no need for this."

In response Kaspar whipped a trash can lid at the elder Hardy. Frank ducked, but the lid ricocheted off the wall behind him and smashed into the back of his shoulders. Frank staggered to his knees. Callie and Iola rushed to help him.

"That does it," Joe said to Kaspar. "You're going down!"

The bouncer came at him again. Joe stepped aside and seized Kaspar's wrist as the bouncer grabbed for him. Joe twisted the big man's arm into a hammerlock and shoved him against the wall.

"I'll get you for this," Kaspar said, snarling. His words were nearly unintelligible because his face was pressed against the bricks.

Phil ran around the corner of the alley. "What's going on?" he asked, taking in the scene. He glanced from Joe to Kaspar, who was still pressed up against the wall. "Is there some kind of problem?"

"Not anymore," Joe said, smiling.

"You know these creeps, Cohen?" Kaspar sputtered. "Get 'em off me!"

"Hey, Joe," Phil said. "Let Geo go. I'm sure this must be some kind of misunderstanding."

Reluctantly Joe let Kaspar go.

"You know this knuckle-breaker, Phil?" the younger Hardy asked.

"Yeah," Phil said. "He usually works backstage. What are you doing out here, Geo?"

Kaspar rubbed his jaw and scowled at Joe. "The regular security guy—Sullivan—had to step away for a minute," he said. "I was filling in when these jerks tried to muscle past me. . . ."

"That's not true," Callie interjected.

"We were just waiting in the alley for you," Iola added. "We tried to tell this guy that, but . . ."

"Maybe I jumped the gun," Kaspar admitted, dusting himself off, "but any crazy fan could claim they were waiting for a friend by the stage entrance."

"Would it have killed you to wait two minutes to find out if we were being honest?" Joe asked, still fuming.

"There are a lot of creeps who want to bother the band," Kaspar said. "Hangers-on, groupies, nutcases . . . you can't blame me for trying to run you off."

"Well," Phil said sternly, "they're with me." He held out his backstage passes for Kaspar to examine.

Kaspar didn't even glance at them. "Yeah, okay. Go on in." He glared angrily at Joe and Frank as the five teens walked through the door into the dimly lit backstage area.

As they entered, the group passed a tall, redheaded teen whose name tag read SULLIVAN. Phil exchanged nods with Sullivan as the regular bouncer relieved Kaspar at the back door. Kaspar sulked off toward the dressing rooms.

"If we'd arrived a couple of minutes later, we could have dealt with someone who knew how to do their job," Iola noted testily.

Phil shrugged. "Geo's job isn't bouncing. He's

part of the road crew—kind of a jack-of-all-trades. He does some sound checks, some lighting, some security, and even plays a few licks on the guitar. Hey, there's Billie Greenberg, the band's manager." Phil waved to a short, frizzy-haired woman who was pacing nervously backstage. She was dressed in a fashionable skirt and blouse, and wore a pair of glasses dangling from a golden chain around her neck.

She smiled and walked toward them, ducking past several busy technicians. "Hey, Phil," she said. "I almost thought you weren't going to make it tonight. Are these your friends?"

Phil nodded. "Joe and Frank Hardy, Callie Shaw, and Iola Morton, meet Billie Greenberg."

The teens took turns shaking hands with Vette Smash's manager. "Pleased to meet you," Frank said.

"Likewise," Ms. Greenberg replied. She glanced at her watch apprehensively. "Have you seen Jackie? We can't go on without her."

"Jackie Rude's the band's drummer," Phil explained. "She likes to arrive at the last minute."

"Enjoys skirting the edge of disaster is more like it," Ms. Greenberg added. "Have you . . . ?"

"Sorry, Ms. Greenberg," Phil said, "I haven't seen her."

"Living life on the edge is unusual for rock stars, isn't it?" Joe asked with a wry smile.

"They're not stars yet," Ms. Greenberg replied.

"And if they blow any of their appearances this week, they may never be." She tapped on the face of her watch, as if hoping it might be broken.

"Are Jewel and the rest of the band members in their dressing rooms?" Phil asked. "I wanted to make some quick intros before the first show."

"You'll have to wait," Ms. Greenberg said. "I don't want anything breaking the band's concentration right now. No offense, Phil."

"None taken," Phil replied, trying his best not to look hurt.

Out front the crowd began chanting, "Vette Smash! Vette Smash!"

"The audience won't wait much longer," Ms. Greenberg said. "We'll have to improvise, see what we can do without Jackie."

She walked to a battered dressing room door and rapped on it three times. The door swung open, revealing two men and one woman—the remaining members of the band.

"That's Julie, known in the band as Chrome Jewel," Phil said, nodding toward a blond girl wearing a chrome outfit and carrying a bass guitar. "Ken Fender's the redhead with the lead guitar. Ray Chong, the dark-haired guy, plays keyboard."

Ken looked around, his eyes narrowing. "Where's Jackie?" he asked.

"MIA," Ms. Greenberg explained. "You'll have to start without her."

15

"Start without drums?" Chrome Jewel asked, incredulous.

"Play a slow ballad or something," Ms. Greenberg suggested.

"Start with a slow number?" Ken replied. "I'd rather die."

"Not on my dime you won't," Ms. Greenberg shot back. "You blow this gig and we're *all* as good as dead. Now get out there and wow them."

The group looked skeptically at their manager, but Billie Greenberg seemed adamant. Reluctantly the trio moved toward the stage.

As if on cue, the backstage door burst open and a skinny woman in a black leather outfit dashed in. She had a streak of purple down the right side of her short-cropped black hair and wore shocking violet contact lenses.

Ray smiled at Jackie Rude, and tossed her a pair of drumsticks. Jackie caught them as they flew and kept going.

"Glad you could make it!" Ms. Greenberg hissed as Jackie whisked past.

The drummer flashed Ms. Greenberg a peace sign and caught up with the others just as they strode through the curtains onto the stage. Bright stage lights blistered the air, glittering off of Vette Smash's flashy attire. For a moment the four band members looked like honest-to-goodness stars, not just up-and-coming locals.

The crowd went wild, shaking the old theater with cheers and stomps. Julie caught Phil's eye and flashed him a quick smile. Then the band kicked into their first song—a hyped-up version of the old classic, "Deadman's Curve."

"Since they're playing two shows tonight," Phil explained to his friends, "I should be able to introduce you to the band between sets."

"Sounds like a plan," Frank said.

The five of them settled back into the wings and enjoyed the show. Technicians bustled around behind the stage, making sure everything ran smoothly during the performance. The Hardys and the others kept out of the crew's way. Several times Kaspar ran past on some errand, but he took no notice of the group.

Vette Smash alternated between radical covers of older tunes, power ballads, and original compositions. Though the brothers and their girlfriends didn't know the new songs, many in the crowd seemed to. Vette Smash's fans sang along to "Dragonman versus Harleyrider," "Once More into the Crusher," "Blood on the Seat Cushions," and the band's theme song, "Last Nightride in Bayport."

Ken played guitar faster with every song as the end of the set drew near. Jewel raced along with him, adding rhythm and counterpoint. Ray pounded the keys so hard that it seemed that they would fly off into the crowd. Jackie was hammering away with her third pair of drumsticks after having broken the first two. Sweat poured down the bodies of all four band members.

Vette Smash struck the final chord of "Hit the Streets," and the stage lights went out. As the crowd's cheers shook the rafters the group raced offstage.

Billie handed them bottles of water, and they guzzled them down. Julie gave Phil a peck on the cheek, then rejoined her friends at the edge of the stage, just out of view of the audience.

"We rocked 'em!" Ken said triumphantly.

"Wait till we hit 'em with the encore," Jewel replied.

"We'll bring this old box tumblin' down," Jackie added.

"Not until the second show, please," Billie said. "Now . . . go!" She pushed the four band members back toward the stage. Kaspar tossed each teen a towel, and they wiped off their faces before dashing out into the blazing spotlights once more.

"You know," Joe said, as the audience thundered their appreciation, "it might be fun to be a rock star."

"Becoming one's the hard part," Frank noted.

Thirty minutes later the band dashed offstage. The Browning's curtains reeled shut, deadening the thunderous applause.

"One down, three to go," Ray noted, pouring bottled water over his head.

"We've got less than an hour before the next set," Ms. Greenberg said. "Grab some food and drink some water. Don't let up for the second crowd. We want the public to know that you're great every time you play."

"Come on," Jackie said to the rest of the band, "let's hit the dressing room while we can."

"Before you go," Phil said, "I'd like to introduce some friends of mine. This is Frank and Joe Hardy, and Callie Shaw and Iola Morton. Guys, meet Ken, Ray, Jackie, and—of course—Chrome Jewel."

"Vette Smash is rocked to meet ya," Ken said, assuming spokesmanship for the band. They all shook hands.

"So, these are the famous Hardy brothers," Jewel/Julie said admiringly. "I've heard a lot about you two."

"Nothing bad, I hope," Joe replied, smirking.

"Aren't you the sons of the famous detective, Fenton Hardy?" Ray asked. "I've read about a lot of his cases."

"That's us," Frank said.

"Well, then maybe you can solve the mystery of why Ken's such a klutz around the equipment," Jackie said, her purple-tinted eyes sparkling.

"Hey, I don't need to be an electronic genius," Ken replied. "That's what we pay the road crew for. I've got my hands full just playing guitar—who has time to learn how to fix one too?"

19

"One day Ken will learn a third chord," Ray said, half-seriously.

Ken laughed. "I gotta crash. Nice meeting you." He raced toward the dressing room.

"You're staying for the second show, aren't you, Phil?" Julie asked.

"Wouldn't miss it," Phil said. "Do the rest of you want to stay too?"

"You bet," Callie and Iola chimed.

"It's not every day you get to hang out with up-and-coming stars," Frank added.

"Smart *and* handsome," Jackie said. "You gals better hold on to those guys, or I may steal one." She laughed and ran toward the dressing room.

"The pace doesn't let up, does it?" Joe said.

"Not until the end of the second show," Ms. Greenberg said. "Enjoy the next set—and be sure to keep out of the way." She bustled off into the wings to talk to some roadies.

As the theater got ready for the second show, the Hardys and their friends snagged some refreshments from a table backstage. Then they settled into some chairs to wait for the second performance.

As showtime drew near once more, Ms. Greenberg dashed up to them, looking almost frantic. "Have you seen the Browning's electrician?" she asked. "We're having trouble with the lights, and we can't find him."

"We haven't seen him," Phil replied. "But I've

20

done all the lighting in the Bayport High productions for the last three years. I could probably fill in if you want me to."

"The union will kill me if they find out," Ms. Greenberg said, "but we can't wait any longer. Go for it, Phil."

Phil nodded and headed up the spiral stairs leading to the big catwalks that ran overhead.

"Don't worry," Frank said. "Phil's a wizard with electronics."

"He'd better be," Ms. Greenberg replied.

A few minutes later the faulty lights flickered back on. Ms. Greenberg smiled. "Just in time!" she said. She rapped on the dressing room door, giving the signal to the band to begin the concert. Julie, now Jewel, and the other band members sprinted onto the stage once more.

Again the crowd went wild, shaking the auditorium with applause. The lights overhead swayed as the noise grew louder.

The Hardys and their girlfriends looked up to where Phil was still working on the lighting. Suddenly Phil lurched over the edge of the catwalk and slipped toward the stage below.

3 The Long Drop

"Phil!" Callie screamed, her voice lost amid the applause.

Phil plunged toward the stage floor, thirty feet below. At the last second, though, he grabbed hold of one of the big braces that helped suspend the banks of lights. He grimaced as the heat of the metal flowed through his hands. Phil still managed to cling to the support and swayed precariously.

Frank and Joe sprinted up the spiral staircase toward the overhead catwalk. Callie and Iola called frantically for assistance. Everyone was so busy backstage, and the band was so loud, that no one heard their pleas.

Phil teetered on the brink of falling. The catwalk rocked precariously with his weight. He reached back toward the railing, but couldn't quite catch hold of it—so he clung desperately to the hot metal brace, trying to find some way out of his predicament.

Frank and Joe raced onto the catwalk.

"Phil! Grab hold!" Frank called. He and Joe thrust their hands toward their friend.

Phil lurched in the brothers' direction. The lights swayed under him like a park swing. Joe and Frank stretched forward and grabbed hold of his wrists. With a mighty heave they pulled Phil off of the lighting apparatus. Phil swung through the air and slammed hard into the side of the catwalk.

"We've got you," Joe said. "We won't let you fall." He and Frank clung tight to Phil's wrists.

Fear filled Phil's eyes and his face was very pale. Sweat poured down his forehead. The lights swayed, brushing Phil's leg. He winced from the heat.

Joe and Frank pulled hard and wrestled their friend over the catwalk's railing. All three of them collapsed into a heap on top of the grating.

"Thanks for saving my bacon," Phil said.

Joe managed a smile. "I thought I smelled something cooking." He looked down at Phil's hands.

"Eh—nothing an ice pack won't cure," Phil said.

"Come on," said Frank, "let's get down from here."

"Down sounds real good," Phil agreed.

The three of them staggered across the walkway and lurched down the stairs to the main floor. Vette

Smash continued to play onstage, oblivious to Phil's near disaster. Iola and Callie ran up and hugged all three boys. Phil had grabbed an ice pack and was nursing his hands.

"I'm okay," Phil said.

"We're all fine," Frank added. "Though I'd rather not do it again."

"No one down here even knew anything was wrong," Callie fumed.

"We tried to get help," Iola said, "but they were all so busy, no one would pay attention to us."

"Life backstage is always pretty hectic," Phil said. "Luckily no harm done—except to my clothes." Dirt, grease, sweat, and scorch marks covered his formerly neat outfit. "My palms are a little cooked too, but they'll be okay."

"What happened up there?" Callie asked. "Did you slip?"

"No," Phil said. "Someone pushed me."

"*What?*" the others blurted simultaneously.

"Yeah. Someone came up from behind and pushed me. I didn't see who it was."

"Why would anyone do that?" Iola asked.

"Good question," said Frank. "Do you have any enemies among the crew?"

Phil shook his head. "No. I get along fine with everyone. The band's been on edge lately, but . . ."

"On edge?" Joe asked. "Why?"

"Well, you saw how things are," Phil replied.

"Everything's getting tougher the closer they get to striking it big. Everybody's tense and worried. I think that's one reason that Jackie shows up late. It's her way of coping. Ken's squawking a lot too. He's even been making noises about a solo career."

"Do you think he's serious?" Callie asked.

"Nah," Phil said. "He's just blowing off steam. I think the possibility of big success scares them all. They're artists, and they have strange ways of dealing with stress."

"But the band's stress level doesn't explain someone pushing you," Frank said. "A fan getting hurt would *not* be good publicity for the band."

"What about Vette Smash's rivals?" Joe asked. "Like those guys who tried to run us off the road earlier?"

"Trying to kill me seems like a pretty extreme tactic for Green Machine fans," Phil said.

"Are you sure you didn't see anyone?" Callie asked.

"I was too busy working on the lights," Phil replied. "I didn't catch a glimpse of whoever did it."

"Are these stairs the only way down from the catwalk?" Joe asked, nodding toward the spiral staircase nearby.

Phil shook his head. "No, there are two or three other exits, including a door onto the roof."

"So it could have been almost anybody coming from anywhere," Frank said. He looked from behind the curtains, out into the packed theater.

"Anybody but the band members," Joe added. "They were all onstage at the time."

Phil sighed and rubbed his head. "This doesn't make any sense. Maybe I just slipped and *imagined* that someone pushed me."

"And you're *so* prone to wild daydreams," Iola said. Her tone was both sarcastic and supportive at the same time.

"I'm going to walk the backstage perimeter," Joe said. "See if I spot anyone suspicious."

"Good idea," Frank agreed. "I'll go in the opposite direction. Callie, you and Iola stay with Phil. Holler if you see anything."

"Over this music? Who would hear us?" Callie asked—but the boys were already out of earshot.

Frank and Joe worked their way around the backstage area. They saw a lot of the band's crew members and stage hands bustling around, but didn't find anything out of the ordinary. On their way back to Phil and the girls, the brothers ran into Ms. Greenberg and two well-dressed people. One was an Asian woman dressed in black. She wore sunglasses, even though they were indoors and it was night. The other stranger was a big, well-dressed man sporting a cowboy hat and a bolo tie embossed with a steer's head.

Ms. Greenberg nodded to the Hardys and smiled nervously at the people with her.

"Anything wrong?" Frank asked.

"Oh, no," Ms. Greenberg replied. "We're just waiting for the end of the show."

"Since Billie here seems disinclined to make introductions," the man said, speaking with a southern accent, "let me do the honors. I'm Walker Crown, and this little filly is Kelly Miyazaki. We're agents looking to represent Vette Smash on the national music scene."

"*Rival* agents," Ms. Miyazaki said, crossing her arms over her chest.

Crown chuckled. "Don't take that rival stuff too seriously," he said. "This is such a close-knit business, we're practically family."

"Family who don't like each other," Ms. Miyazaki added.

Crown laughed again. Ms. Greenberg chuckled nervously.

"Frank and Joe Hardy," Frank said. He and Joe shook hands with the agents.

"They're friends of Vette Smash," Ms. Greenberg explained.

Crown smiled. "Good. Everybody needs friends. Especially friends who will stick by you when the road to stardom gets rocky. Friends like . . ."

"Like the *Crown Agency*," Ms. Miyazaki said, finishing his sentence for him. "You'll have to forgive Walker. He's always selling something. We're both pleased to meet you, I'm sure."

"Why don't we grab something from the refreshment table," Ms. Greenberg suggested. "Then I'll find us a place to relax until the show's over."

"Any place is fine with me," Crown said. "Why, back on my ranch, I once sat on a rock for three days. . . ." His words trailed off as he and Ms. Miyazaki followed Ms. Greenberg behind a backstage curtain and out of sight.

"That's quite a trio," Joe said after they'd gone.

"No love lost between those agents," Frank said. "Ms. Greenberg may need a referee's license to keep them apart. She looks pretty nervous about it."

Joe shrugged. "She's got a lot on the line. Everyone here does."

The Hardys rejoined Phil and the girls, and the five of them hung out and relaxed during the rest of the set.

Vette Smash played with frenetic intensity all the way through their final encore. Kaspar tossed them all cold towels as they sprinted offstage for the last time.

Once out from under the spotlights, the band once again mopped their faces and caught their breaths. The noise beyond the curtains gradually died away as the crowd left the theater and the Browning's crew began cleaning up.

"Two shows, two slam dunks," Ken said, sweat dripping from his brow. Kaspar handed him a bottle of water, and the band's leader downed it in one long gulp. Julie drank her water more slowly, while Ray and Jackie poured some of theirs over their heads.

"Great concerts," Phil said. "You all sounded super tonight."

"What'd you say?" Ray asked in an exaggerated, loud voice. "I can't hear anything after playing two amazingly loud sets."

Everyone laughed.

As the band recovered, Ms. Greenberg bustled in alone, but still looking nervous.

"Kelly Miyazaki and Walker Crown are here to see you," she told the band. "They're talking about national representation for Vette Smash. I think we can play them off against each other and get a really good deal. You put on a great show tonight, and I hope you're up to showing these agents what you're made of. Ready?"

"No," said Ken. The rest of the band echoed his assessment.

"Look, we're grateful they've come to see us," Jackie said, "but we're beat. We just played two concerts with barely an hour in between them. Can you at least give us a couple of minutes before the vultures start circling?"

"They're not vultures; they're your *future*," Ms. Greenberg said testily.

"Well, our future can wait about fifteen minutes, can't it?" Julie asked. "You don't want us to look like beat-down dogs, do you?"

Ken and Ray nodded their agreement. "We'll get to 'em, Billie," Ken said. "Just give us some time to recover and pull our act together."

Ms. Greenberg made a sour face. "Agents this powerful don't like to be kept waiting, you know. We're lucky that they even came to the show."

"There are always more agents," Ray said flippantly.

"Not tonight there aren't," Ms. Greenberg replied. "Straighten yourselves up, relax for a couple of minutes, then put on your game faces. This could be the most important evening of your careers. I'll stall them for a couple of minutes, then bring them back."

Ken sighed. "Yeah, okay."

"Be ready," Ms. Greenberg said.

"Yes, Mom," Julie said. The rest of the band laughed.

After Ms. Greenberg had gone, Iola said, "A bit pushy, huh?"

"She's a manager," Frank replied. "It's her job to be pushy."

"And she's right," Phil added. "This could be the band's big break. Miyazaki and Crown represent some huge national acts. Vette Smash can't afford to mess up this chance."

"Sounds like Phil here wants to be our new manager," Ken said.

"Maybe he can pick up your act after we kick you out," Ray jibed.

Ken glared at the keyboard player. "After I dump you losers, you mean."

Julie rolled her eyes. "Let's hit the dressing room and relax for a moment before the agents start circling. Come on, Phil. You and your friends can join us."

The five teens followed Vette Smash into the dressing room complex. There was a large common room, six smaller curtained-off cubicles to the sides, and an adjoining shower area and bathroom in the rear. The accommodations weren't the most modern, but the space was much larger than the Hardys had imagined looking from the outside.

Band gear lay strewn around the room: spare instrument parts, pieces of costumes and street clothing, and other personal items belonging to the band. A phone and answering machine sat in one corner of the room beside a TV and a small portable stereo.

Julie and the others took a few minutes to change and freshen up. When they'd finished, they returned to the common area and flopped onto some director's chairs and a battered couch.

"It looks like you guys got a message," Joe said, noticing the flashing light on the answering machine. "Want me to play it?"

"Sure," Ken said.

Joe pressed the button and the message rewound. Then a deep, menacing voice echoed from the machine.

"This is a friend," the voice said, though it sounded anything but friendly. "If you know what's good for you, you'll lay low and avoid showy publicity. Otherwise you might get hurt."

4 Dial-a-Threat

Stunned silence filled the dressing room as the message ended and the machine clicked off.

Jackie stood up and stretched. "Another wrong number," she said lightly.

"Ken, you've got to tell your mom to stop calling," Ray joked. He turned to the others. "She always worries about him."

"Cut the comedy, you guys," Phil said. "That sounded like a serious threat to me."

"We get crank calls all the time," Julie said. "It's probably one of those local radio station stunts."

"Well, if it was, it wasn't a very funny one," Joe said.

"Nobody likes being the butt end of a joke," Ken

said. "I don't think it's worth worrying about, though."

"What's not worth worrying about?" Ms. Greenberg asked as she entered the room.

"Nothing," Ken replied.

"Someone left a threatening message on the answering machine," Callie said. Ken shot her a nasty look.

Ms. Greenberg played the message back, then frowned. "Well, I'm glad you all think this is funny," she said, "but I don't. Some people take the local music scene very seriously, you know."

"Like that girl who shaved Ken's initials into her hair," Jackie said.

"I'm not just talking about loopy fans," Ms. Greenberg replied. "Dick Devlin and his band, Green Machine, would love to see you fall on your faces. You've got two agents interested in you. Green Machine would kill to have that kind of attention. There's no telling what they—or their fans—might do."

"Lighten up, Billie," Ken replied. "It's just a prank—something to throw us off our game."

"Yeah," Ray said. "Whoever left the message probably meant us to hear it before the show."

"Too bad the answering machine doesn't have a time stamp," Joe mused.

Frank nodded. "That could indicate whether Ray is right or not."

"I refuse to be spooked," Julie said. "We've had a big night, and we've got a huge day ahead of us tomorrow. So let's enjoy ourselves while we can. Right, Phil?"

"Yeah, okay."

"Good," Ken said. "Now, when are the corporate leeches showing up?"

"You got me so flustered that I almost forgot," Ms. Greenberg said. "You've got about five minutes. Sullivan's showing them the week's event schedule right now. I have to get back before they miss me. But, *please,* no talk of leeches when I bring them in, okay? Miyazaki and Crown may not be the most pleasant people, but we need them."

"Right," Jackie said wryly.

"I say we open up the bidding and go with whoever comes out on top," said Ray.

"Or they could just slug it out," Julie suggested, smirking.

"We can talk about how to pick between them later," Ms. Greenberg said. "For now, prepare yourselves—and behave." She bustled out of the room, almost bumping into Kaspar on her way out.

"I brought some post-concert food," Kaspar said, pushing a tray table piled high with refreshments. "Where do you want it?"

"Anywhere," Ken said. "Everybody, dig in."

Kaspar parked the cart in an empty corner of the

35

room and everyone dug in. The band members ate as if they hadn't seen food in days.

"Performing works up an appetite, I guess," Callie whispered to her friends.

"From the way they sweat, playing must burn off a lot of calories," Iola agreed.

Kaspar left and for several minutes, the slurps and munches dominated the room. Then the dressing room door squeaked open, and Ms. Miyazaki entered the room—alone. "Evening, all," she said. She introduced herself to the band members and shook everyone's hand.

"Weren't Ms. Greenberg and Mr. Crown supposed to be coming with you?" Frank asked.

"They got tied up," Ms. Miyazaki replied. She smiled and addressed the band. "I'm sure you're wondering why my agency is best suited to represent you. Miyazaki Management is an international agenting firm, with representatives on three continents. Mr. Crown, however, is only a national rep."

"I think I'll describe my own services, if you don't mind," Crown drawled as he entered the room. "You're a slippery little kitten, Kelly. Me and Billie have been lookin' everywhere for you for the past five minutes."

Miyazaki smiled insincerely. "No law against a lady getting a leg up on her competition."

Crown returned the grin. "Well, whatever she's

told you, don't believe half of it," he said to the band. "I, on the other hand, am the real deal."

The agents talked, point and counterpoint, for the better part of twenty minutes. As Crown and Miyazaki finished their presentations, the band looked even more bleary-eyed and exhausted than they had right after the concert.

Ken rubbed his temples. "Thanks for talking to us," he said. "Give us some time to think about it?"

"Yeah, some time when our brains aren't fried from exhaustion," Jackie added.

"Well, my offer isn't open forever," Ms. Miyazaki said.

"Mine either," said Crown.

"We just need a couple of days," Ms. Greenberg said quickly. "That will give you both some time to see the band in action, too. We've got a big publicity event sceduled for tomorrow."

"That bridge bungee jump?" Crown asked. "I read about that in the paper."

Joe and Frank turned to each other and mouthed, "Bungee jump?"

Ms. Greenberg smiled. "Yes, we're promoting the band's new number, 'I Would Dive for You.' It's already gotten a lot of media attention."

"Local media," Crown added.

"It's an interesting stunt," Miyazaki said. "We'll see how it works out."

"Great," Julie said, sounding nearly as tired as she looked. "See you all tomorrow, then."

"Assuming I can squeeze it into my schedule," Ms. Miyazaki said. "I'm talking to some other local bands, as well."

"I'll try to make time," Crown said. He tipped his hat to the ladies and headed out the door. "Catch you later." Miyazaki nodded curtly and followed him out.

"Could that have been any more dull and tiring?" Jackie asked once they'd gone.

"Jackie, that's your *future* walking out that door," Ms. Greenberg said, exasperated. "Try to show some more respect." She sighed. "All of you, get some rest. I'll see you at the jump tomorrow." Vette Smash's manager hurried out of the room. The door swung shut behind her, but it didn't latch.

A minute later two fans tried to push their way in. "We love you, Jewel!" one of the guys yelled.

Frank leaped up and put his shoulder to the door before the fans could barge into the dressing room. "Security!" Ken yelled. A few moments later, Sullivan and Kaspar came and muscled the fans out of the building.

"Phew!" Iola sighed. "So that's who Geo thought we were before. Yikes."

"It can be rough, sometimes," Julie said.

"Well, I've had enough of our adoring public for one day," Ken said. "Once the guards clear the place out, I'm splitting."

"Not heading home to rest, I'll bet," Jackie said, her purple contact lenses making her eyes twinkle.

"Nah," Ken replied. "The roadhouse out by the highway is open until two. Who's in?"

Jackie, Ray, and Julie quickly agreed. "What about the rest of you?" Julie asked.

"It's a school night," Frank said.

"And we need our beauty rest," Joe added.

"That goes for us girls too," Callie said.

"Though we obviously need less beauty sleep than these lugs," Iola said. She gave Joe a playful tap on the arm.

"School for me, too, I'm afraid," Phil said. "I'll be with you in spirit, though."

"I'm sure you will," Julie said, giving him a kiss on the cheek.

Ray opened the door a crack and peered out. "I think the coast is clear," he said. "Who wants to take point?"

"We will," Frank offered. "We'll let you know if anyone's lurking around. Come on, guys." He led Joe and the others out through the darkened theater. They reached the back door without seeing anyone. "All clear!" he called to the band before he and the others stepped into the darkness.

The night had turned wet since the time they entered the theater. A persistent, drizzling rain misted the cool evening air.

Callie shivered. "I wish I'd brought a coat," she said.

"It's only a couple of blocks," Frank said, putting his arm around her waist.

"You could wait in the theater while I get the car," Phil offered.

"No, that's okay," Iola said. "We won't melt."

"Ms. Miyazaki might," Joe said. "She looked pretty witchlike in that black outfit!"

"It was pretty tricky—the way she slipped away from Greenberg and tried to outfox Crown," Callie said. "Though I don't think I'd call it *magical.*"

"Miyazaki has a reputation for being ruthless," Phil said. "I've heard she's done some shady things in the past. Ms. Greenberg says she's one of the best in the business, though."

"I don't think I'd want to be part of a business in which you have to jump off a bridge to get attention," Iola said. "Vette Smash may be up to it, but that's a little extreme for my taste."

Frank rubbed his chin. "I wonder if tomorrow's bungee jump ties in with that threatening phone message."

"Jumping off a bridge is definitely a showy publicity stunt," Joe admitted.

"I think Ken was probably right," Phil said. "That phone call was just an attempt to throw Vette Smash off their game."

"Making them nervous could be especially

effective with two big agents lurking around," Callie noted.

"And if Vette Smash screws up," Iola said, "that might give another band a chance to sign with either Crown or Miyazaki. Do you think Green Machine could be behind a prank like this?"

"Well, one of their fans did throw that bottle at Phil's car earlier," Joe said.

Callie suddenly stopped dead in her tracks. "Oh! I just realized," she said. "I left my purse in Vette Smash's dressing room."

"No problem," Frank said. "I'll run back and get it. You guys keep going. No sense in having *all* of us getting wetter."

"Okay," Phil said. "We'll grab the car and meet you out in front of the theater."

"Sounds like a plan," Frank replied.

He turned and dashed back the way they'd come, while the others continued on to Phil's car. As Frank jogged toward the Browning, it began to rain harder.

The elder Hardy increased his pace. Frank participated in cross-country events at Bayport High, so running through bad weather didn't faze him. As the storm built into a downpour he remained focused on his pace and his footing. He ran up to the Browning's front door, but it was locked—and he didn't see anyone inside to let him in.

He darted around back to the stage entrance. As

he jogged through the narrow side alley he heard a conversation echoing around the corner.

"There isn't enough room in Bayport for two up-and-coming bands," a voice said. "If Green Machine is going to make it big, Vette Smash has to go."

5 Songs from the Shadows

Frank stopped, straining to hear the conversation above the sound of the falling rain. The echoes in the alley distorted the voices so they were difficult to understand.

". . . agree that's the only way it will work . . ." said one voice. Frank missed the rest of the sentence in the din.

". . . short of an accident or an act of . . ."

Frank crept toward the entrance to the backstage alley. He peeked around the corner, but saw no one near the battered door. The voices didn't grow any louder or more recognizable, either.

"Isn't that pretty extreme?"

"Some people will do anything to put their group on top. You have to ask yourself . . ."

43

Frank realized that the acoustics of the alley were affecting the sound. Perhaps the weather was amplifying the echoes too. The plotters, whoever they were, might be around the next corner, or they might be another half block away. Frank couldn't tell. He inched along the back wall of the next building toward what he assumed was the source of the conversation.

". . . willing to do whatever it takes. My group needs to come out on top. . . ."

"That's what I wanted to hear. . . ."

"So what's the next step?"

As Frank concentrated on deciphering the conversation, he didn't notice a box of cans for recycling pushed up against the wall near his feet. The crate overturned and, with a crash, the cans spilled out across the alley. Frank froze, hoping the noise wouldn't give him away.

"What was that?"

"I don't know."

". . . someone listening?"

"Maybe."

". . . can't conclude this right now . . . pick up our conversation later."

"All right. I'll call you. . . ."

The conversation ceased and the sound of hurried footsteps echoed in the darkness.

Frank cursed his own clumsiness and ran full tilt around the nearest corner. He skidded into a big puddle, barely keeping his balance. He swiftly grabbed on to the corner of the building and stopped, peering into the driving rain.

Vague shadows loomed out of the darkness. The buildings around the old theater formed a maze of alleys; presenting numerous hiding places and avenues of escape.

Did the conspirators go down one of these streets? Or are they right around the corner? Frank thought.

Seeing no one, Frank reversed course, splashed through the big puddle again, and headed for the nearest street corner. He covered the distance quickly and did a sharp turn onto the sidewalk running beside Kifflie Avenue.

Near the alley's entrance, a woman was stooping next to her car. Frank didn't see her until it was almost too late.

He put on the brakes, but his sneakers didn't grip the wet pavement very well. Frank hopped to one side and spun—barely avoiding hitting the woman. He tumbled into a wide puddle beside the curb with a resounding splash.

"Are you all right?" the woman asked. As she turned, Frank recognized Ms. Greenberg's surprised face.

Frank got up and wrung out his shirttails. "Nothing a blow-dryer won't fix," he said.

Ms. Greenberg peered questioningly at him.

"You're one of those Hardy boys, aren't you? What are you doing here?"

"My girlfriend forgot her purse at the theater," Frank said. "I came back for it."

"But you're going in the wrong direction," Ms. Greenberg noted.

"The front door was locked," Frank said, thinking fast. "I heard someone talking and thought it might be one of the theater people, on their way home. Have you seen anyone around?"

"Nobody but me," she replied. "And I'm sorry, but I don't have a key to the theater. Now, if you'll excuse me, I'd like to get out of the rain." She got into her car and drove away, pausing only long enough to call, "Good luck rescuing that purse."

"Thanks," Frank called back. He watched her taillights vanish into the rain, then hiked dejectedly to the back of the theater.

The back door was locked too, but a janitor opened it in response to Frank's persistent knocking. Ten minutes later, Callie's purse in hand, the elder Hardy met his friends out front.

"What took you so long?" Joe asked.

"You're drenched!" Callie exclaimed.

Frank explained what he'd overheard and the brief chase that followed the conversation.

"Should we go back and check the area again?" Iola asked.

Frank shook his head. "It's no use. Whoever they were, they're long gone by now."

"Do you think Billie Greenberg was one of the people you heard talking?" Phil asked.

"Maybe," Frank said. "It was impossible to identify the voices because of the downpour and the echoes in the alleyway. I couldn't even be sure where the voices were coming from. What they were saying sounded pretty suspicious, though."

Phil turned the car onto Racine Street and headed toward home. "It seems pretty clear that someone is out to mess things up for Vette Smash," he said. "The question is, who?"

"Green Machine and their supporters seem the obvious suspects," Joe said.

"We'll have to gather some more information on them," Frank agreed.

"Maybe this is just a one-time problem, though," Callie said. "We can certainly hope it is."

"Let's hope," Joe replied, "but let's be prepared."

The next day the Vette Smash concerts made the morning papers, both because of what had happened inside the hall and for an incident outside. A publicity van had driven down the street before the second show, blaring Green Machine songs. This had annoyed the waiting Vette Smash fans. Some of them had pelted the van with bottles and trash.

Police and security quickly broke up the trouble before it could turn chaotic. The way the news played the story, it was debatable whether the incident cast the fans of Green Machine or Vette Smash's admirers in a worse light. The papers didn't mention Phil's accident, as the Hardys and their friends hadn't told anyone.

Frank, Joe, and the rest of the teens had an unremarkable day in school. They kept their ears sharp for any signs of trouble, but nothing related to Vette Smash cropped up.

"One thing's for sure," Iola said after school. "The fans of the two bands don't like one another very much."

"Didn't you hear?" Frank asked, smiling. "There isn't room enough in Bayport for two up-and-coming bands. A little birdy told me that."

"So you're thinking that rabid fans are behind the trouble last night both outside the theater *and* inside?" Callie asked.

"That makes sense," Joe said. "Phil falling from the rafters during a show couldn't help Vette Smash. Someone getting hurt at a concert is never good publicity."

"Pushing someone from a catwalk is a pretty extreme measure to take," Frank said. "If you wanted to mess up the show, it'd be much easier to start a big brawl in the audience."

"Much easier to catch the perps too," Joe noted.

Frank frowned. "There's some piece of this case we're not seeing yet."

"Let's hope this isn't a case at all," Callie said. "I don't know how the two of you stand chasing criminals all the time."

Joe shrugged. "Someone's got to do it."

"But it didn't leave you much time to relax and enjoy the music," Iola noted.

They caught up with Phil in the parking lot after school.

"I'm surprised you aren't getting ready for Vette Smash's bungee jump," Frank said. "Isn't it taking place in about an hour from now?"

"Forty-five minutes," Phil said glumly. "But I have to pick up some gear for tonight's show. I'm meeting the band after the jump, so I'm going to miss the actual stunt."

"Too bad," Joe said. "I'm sure you'll be able to catch the replay on the news tonight, though."

"Let's hope so," Phil said. "If not, the band's taking a big risk for nothing. Hey, you want to help me out?"

"Sure," Frank said. "How?"

"Loading the band's gear into my car would take at least two trips," Phil said. "If we used your van, though, we could make it in one. We'd still miss the jump, probably, but at least we could hang out afterward. The band's last two shows are tonight. Want to go?"

"Sounds good," Joe said. "I don't think Frank or I have gotten tired of being 'with the band' yet."

"Though we'll be happier if you stay out of the spotlight tonight, Phil," Frank added, grinning. "What about you girls?"

Iola shook her head. "I promised I'd run some homework and supplies out to Chet at the farm."

"And I promised to keep her company," Callie said.

"Chet doing work-study *and* homework?" Joe said in mock surprise. "What's the world coming to?"

"We'll catch you tomorrow, then," Frank said.

"Be sure of it," Callie replied, giving him a peck on the cheek. "Steer clear of those Green Machine fanatics."

"Hey," Joe said, "they better steer clear of *us*."

Iola rolled her eyes. "That's just what Callie and I are worried about."

"Don't fret," Phil said, "I'll keep your boyfriends out of trouble."

The girls headed off to Iola's to hunt for Chet's supplies. The Hardys dropped Phil's car off at his house, then took the van out to the band's storage shed to pick up Vette Smash's equipment.

"This place looks like an electronics warehouse," Joe remarked as they swung open the storage unit's big doors.

"Yeah," Phil said. "The band's accumulated a lot of gear over the last few months."

"So, which of this stuff are we loading?" Frank asked.

"Some mixing boards to start," Phil said. "The band wasn't happy with the sound we got at the Browning last night. Let's also pack a couple of big fans to cool off the stage area. Oh, and the lightning generators."

Joe arched his eyebrows. "Lightning generators?"

"It's a new special effect Vette Smash is trying out," Phil said. He indicated several towering black boxes topped with huge metallic globes. "These make big chains of electricity arc over the band as they play."

"And here I thought concerts were about music," Frank said, laughing.

"You've got to sell fans the sizzle before they buy the steak," Phil replied.

"Hey, check this out," Joe said, holding up a set of long black cords that smelled like old rubber bands. "Don't they need these for the bungee jump? I thought they were doing it right now."

"They are," Phil said. "That's one of the band's spares. They've been practicing this stunt for weeks."

"Hey, Frank, catch," Joe said, tossing one end of the bungee cord to his older brother.

Frank grabbed the far end of the cord, and the two brothers engaged in an impromptu tug-of-war.

"How far do these things stretch?" Frank asked.

"I think two or three times their original size

before they snap back," Phil said. "But I'm no expert. The band had them sized by professionals for this bridge jump. If they're too long, you'll hit the ground; too short, and you could crack your neck with whiplash from the sudden stop."

"Sounds dangerous," Joe said. "Oof!"

He and Frank flew back through the air, crashing into opposite walls of the storage shed.

"Are you guys okay?" Phil asked.

"We're fine," Joe said. He and Frank got up and rubbed their backsides.

"Good thing the band wasn't using *this* cord today. It's obviously defective." Joe held up the broken ends of the long rubber cord. The bungee they were tugging had snapped in two.

Frank's brown eyes narrowed. "This bungee cord didn't break," he said. "It's been *cut*!"

6 Cutting the Chords

"Are you sure?" Phil asked.

"Look at the ends," Frank said. "See how half the break is straight and the other half is ragged? Someone severed this bungee halfway, so that it would snap."

"But who would . . . ?" Joe began.

"Doesn't matter right now," Phil said. "The cords the group is using came from here. Their bungees may be sabotaged just like this one. They could be jumping to their deaths!"

"Not if we can help it," Frank said. "Let's go!"

He, Phil, and Joe raced to the Hardys' van and zoomed away. Joe plotted the quickest route to the jump location while Frank drove. Phil attempted to reach the band on his cell phone.

"Great time to have no signal!" he said, snarling.

"Keep trying," Frank said. "It might get stronger as we go." He turned left on Hebert Boulevard, taking the back roads toward the abandoned Northwestern railroad trestle.

A few tense minutes passed as they raced down the road while Phil punched numbers into the cell phone. "Now I'm getting their voice mail!" he said.

"All of them?" Joe asked.

"Julie's, Ken's, Ms. Greenberg's—yeah, the whole lot," Phil said, frustrated. "They must have turned their phones off to avoid being distracted during the setup for the jump."

"Try the cops, then—and the news media," Joe suggested. "Maybe someone can get there before we can."

"The media must already have reporters on the bridge," Frank said. "They have to be covering the dive, otherwise, why jump?"

"Good thought," Phil said. He called up directory assistance, then punched in the numbers for WBPT and several other media outlets.

"I told them," he said, after he'd finished, "but I'm not sure any of them believed me. They wouldn't let me talk directly to the remote trucks."

"What about the police?" Joe asked.

"They're sending someone out," Phil replied. "They have off-duty patrolmen working security on the jump, but they weren't sure they'd be able to reach them right away."

"We're almost there," Frank said. "Hang on!"

He skidded the van off of the main road and onto the dirt trail leading down to the tracks. This branch of the Northwestern line had been abandoned for years, but the railroad's big iron-and-timber bridge still stretched over Scott's Gorge.

Because it was a bridge built only for trains, cars had no access to the old trestle. Frank stopped the van in the dirt roundabout near the top of the bluff.

"Shoot!" he said. "I was hoping some of the TV vans might be parked here. They could have radioed to their people on the tracks, and had them stop the jump."

"The media must have parked on the other side of the gorge," Joe said. "We'll just have to make a run for it." They all hopped out of the van and sprinted downhill toward the rusting railroad tracks.

They soon spotted the band, surrounded by a big collection of media people in the middle of the bridge. A group of onlookers had gathered on the far side of the span, lining the rolling bluff on top of Scott's Gorge.

The Hardys and Phil ran toward the bridge, waving their arms and shouting, "Stop! Stop!" The people on the rusting trestle paid no attention, mistaking the three teens for excited onlookers.

The three friends ran smack into Sullivan, the big bouncer, at the end of the bridge. "No fans allowed on . . ." he began. Then, noticing Phil, he smiled. "Oh, it's you. I didn't think you were going to make it."

"Those bungees may have been sabotaged!" Phil blurted.

Sullivan looked stunned. "What?"

"A spare bungee cord from the set had been cut," Frank said. "The band members may be jumping to their doom!" Phil and Joe kept running while Frank explained.

Sullivan pulled a walkie-talkie from his belt, but he was nervous, and the receiver slipped through his fingers. The radio bounced off of a railroad tie, sailed over the edge of the bridge, and smashed on the rocks at the bottom of the gorge. Sullivan ran after the Hardys and Phil.

In the center of the aging span, Ken walked to the edge of the rail and raised his hands high in the air. "I would dive for you!" he said, looking straight into the cluster of cameras gathered around the group.

Julie, Jackie, and Ray all raised their hands in imitation of Vette Smash's lead singer. "I would dive for you!" they repeated.

They turned as a group and stepped onto the top of the guardrail.

"Stop! Stop!" Phil and Joe shouted.

"Those bungees have been cut!" Frank yelled.

For a moment the band members tottered atop the railing as they spotted the three teens running toward them. Julie, Jackie, and Ray all stepped back. Ken, though, seemed on the verge of losing his balance.

Just in time Joe lunged forward and grabbed the back of Ken's pants as the singer was about to fall over the edge. With a mighty heave Joe pulled Ken back to safety. The two of them landed hard on the bridge's wooden floorbeams.

"What's going on here?" Ms. Greenberg said, rushing forward.

"We were checking the equipment at the storage shed," Phil explained, "and discovered that one of the remaining bungees had been cut."

"We tried to call you," Frank said, "but couldn't get through." As he spoke, flashing police lights appeared at the top of the ridge on the far side of the trestle.

"That's crazy," Julie said. "Who would want to cut our bungee cords?"

Intrigued, the media pressed in closer around the group for the event. Flashbulbs flashed and film cameras rolled as microphones leaned in to catch the conversation.

"Are you sure about this?" Ms. Greenberg asked.

"Let's take a look," Frank said. He, Joe, and Phil began to systematically examine the cords attached to the jumpers' backs. They tugged sharply on each of the thick elastic bands. As they pulled, Ken's bungee gave a resounding *snap*.

The assembled crowd gasped.

"No way!" Ken said. "No freaking way!" He turned angrily on the rest. "I put myself on the line every night, and someone does *this* to me?"

"Hey, it's not just you," Julie said. "We chose those cords at random. Any one of us could have been hurt."

"Yeah," Ken said, "but *I'm* the one who got the bad bungee." He glared at the whole crowd. "I don't know who's responsible for this, but whoever you are, you're on my list!"

Ken threw off his bungee harness and stalked down the tracks toward the parking lot on the far side of the bridge. He shoved Kaspar out of his way as he went, and the guard almost fell over the rail. The rest of the band watched in frustration as Ken climbed the short hill to the parking area, then sped away in his red sports car.

"Don't worry," Ray said. "He'll settle down in time for tonight's show." None of the others seemed convinced. The news reporters pressed in and started asking questions.

Ms. Greenberg stood off to one side, looking especially worried. She ran her hands through her frizzy hair and moaned. "This isn't a publicity stunt, it's a disaster!"

"I wouldn't be too sure about that, darlin'," Walker Crown said. The big Texan came down the bluff side by side with Kelly Miyazaki. Crown looked pleased; Miyazaki did not.

"Walker is from the 'any publicity is good publicity' school," Ms. Miyazaki said. "I, on the other hand, agree with Ms. Greenberg—this is a disaster."

Crown scoffed. "It's nothing I couldn't turn around in a New York minute—assuming Vette Smash signs with me." He flashed a perfect smile at the band. "Stand back and watch the master at work."

He strode into the crowd of reporters, cutting them off from the band, and began speaking. "Now, now," Crown said. "Y'all know how ruthless the local music scene can be. It's clear that *someone* doesn't want Vette Smash climbing their way to the top of the charts." He continued in that vein, the press hanging on his every word.

"Windbag," Ms. Miyazaki whispered to Ms. Greenberg. "You know where to reach me when you need to sort out the mess he's made. I wouldn't let him carry on too much, if I were you." She turned on her heel and walked up the hill to the nearby lot.

"I just can't win!" Ms. Greenberg muttered.

As Crown spoke the band members edged away from the crowd. "At least Crown got us out of that feeding frenzy," Julie said to her friends. "You think we can leave without stirring them back up?"

"We could give you a ride," Joe offered. "The press are all parked on the other side of the ravine."

"Sounds great," said Julie. "The three of us rode here with Billie, anyway."

"Billie, cover our escape, will you?" Jackie asked.

Vette Smash's manager nodded. "All right. It's the least I can do. I'll see you tonight."

The band members, the Hardys, and Phil all hustled off the trestle and up the ridge to the Hardys' van.

"Thanks for keeping us from going splat, Phil," Jackie said. "We appreciate it."

"Some people dug our misfortune, though," Ray said. "I spotted Dick Devlin and some of the Green Machine supporters on the other side of the tracks. They were having a grand old time."

"Devlin's the Green Machine's manager, isn't he?" Joe asked. He slid behind the wheel of the van and drove them out of the parking area.

"Yeah, and Devlin's a good name for him," Julie said. "He's been devilin' us since we signed with Billie."

"She may not be the swiftest manager," Jackie said, "but at least she's honest."

"Devlin's hands are dirtier than an Indy 500 pit crew's," Ray added.

"I don't know why his band is popular," Phil said.

"Scanty costumes," Julie suggested.

"Big noise," Jackie added.

"Bribes," Ray finished. "So, where are we headed?"

"We still have to pick up the equipment from the shed," Phil said. "We didn't have time to grab anything after we found out the bungees had been sabotaged."

"After we get the gear, we could rustle up some food before the concert, if you want," Frank said.

"Don't bother," Jackie replied. "They always have a decent spread laid out for us backstage."

"It's in our contract," Ray added.

"Why pay when you can eat for free?" Julie asked.

The six of them picked up the equipment from the storage shed. Then the Hardys dropped off Ray and Jackie so they could pick up their own cars. Julie decided to ride with Phil and the Hardys. They all headed downtown to the Browning. Kaspar was manning the stage door when they arrived, but they didn't have any trouble with him this time. He even smiled and bowed as he opened the door.

"From obnoxious to obsequious in one easy lesson," Joe whispered to Frank.

"Phil told me about your run-in with Geo last night," Julie said. "He's overly enthusiastic sometimes, but usually he's really helpful."

"I'll have him help carry in the equipment, then," Phil said wryly. He headed back toward the van.

The Hardys and Julie found Ray and Jackie at the refreshment table. They all enjoyed the food, though the members of the band ate lightly.

"We eat like birds," Ray explained, "small portions, almost fifteen times a day. It keeps our energy up."

The Hardys chatted with the band and the crew. Phil helped the technical staff set up the lightning generators. Then Vette Smash gave the equipment a dress rehearsal. Kaspar stood in for Ken, who was still missing in action.

"He's pretty good," Frank noted.

"On guitar, he's got talent," Phil agreed. "Lucky Ken's out, and not Ray. No one in the crew can play keyboard."

"What about drums?" Joe asked.

"Well, I've heard Geo and some of the other roadies try," Phil said. "Let's just say that they're a little . . . off beat." He grinned, and the brothers laughed.

Ms. Greenberg paced nervously as the time for the first show drew near.

Two minutes before curtain Ken barged in through the stage doorway. He grabbed his guitar and, without a word to anyone, headed for the stage. Ms. Greenberg let out an audible sigh of relief. The rest of Vette Smash followed their leader onto the stage.

Despite the last-minute arrival, the first show went without a hitch. Fake lightning flashed overhead, and the band rocked the house. At the end of the set even Billie Greenberg was smiling.

The band grabbed a quick bite while the crew cleaned up the theater and prepared for the next show. Soon audience members for the second set began filtering in.

Just before the curtain was due to go up, Phil pulled Frank and Joe aside. "See that tall guy in the black T-shirt?" he asked, pointing to a blond teen with spiky hair. "That's Todd 'Grodd' Green, leader of Green Machine—without his trademark green wig. Dick Devlin is the bruiser standing next to him."

"Maybe they just came to catch the show," Joe said.

"Or maybe this is another attempt to throw Vette Smash off their game," Frank suggested.

"More likely, they heard we were using some new special effects tonight and wanted to scout them out," Phil said. "They're always trying to top whatever Vette Smash does."

"They'll have a hard time beating that lightning generator," Joe said. "It's spectacular."

"Comin' through!" Jackie shouted. Phil and the brothers stepped back as Jackie and the rest of Vette Smash stormed back onto the stage.

They opened the second set with "Once More into the Crusher," before rocking right into "I Would Dive for You," and then followed with a blazing cover of "Riders on the Storm."

That was the cue for the lightning machine, and everyone in the house looked up, anticipating the display. The big generators whirred to life and sparks began to fly.

Instead of arcing in between the two electrodes, though, a huge bolt of electricity suddenly shot toward the band.

7 Lightning Rods

"Hit the deck!" Ken yelled.

The band members dove to the floor as sparks rained around them. Lightning zapped over their heads toward the audience.

The concert-goers screamed and leaped for cover. One of the bolts hit a row of chairs and set the seat cushions on fire. The audience fled toward the exit, nearly trampling one another in their haste to escape.

"Stay low!" Frank called as the members of Vette Smash scrambled to get off the stage.

Julie's metallic costume sparkled in the glow of the artificial lightning strikes. As she crept toward the wings, a flash of electricity hit her between the shoulder blades. Julie pitched forward onto the stage, unconscious.

"Julie!" Phil cried.

"Shut that thing down," Joe said. "We'll rescue Julie."

He and Frank shuffled forward in a crouch, keeping their contact with the ground as minimal as possible, while Phil ran to stop the lightning machine.

The fire in the seats was spreading, but with the lightning raging overhead, no one dared to come back into the room to extinguish it.

Bolts flashed from the tall generators to the stage, barely missing Julie's prone body.

"I don't think she's badly hurt," Joe said as he and Frank reached her.

"Let's drag her out of here before we're all cooked," Frank said. "Watch the metal on her costume. It's like she's wearing a lightning rod."

"Tell me something I *don't* know," Joe said. As quickly as they could, the two teens dragged Julie off the stage. As they went, the noise of the lightning machine built to a deafening whine.

"Don't look now," Frank said, "but I think that generator is going to blow."

Smoke and sparks billowed from the metallic globes that topped the generator towers. An acrid smell filled the air.

"Brace yourself!" Joe said, wishing they'd gotten farther away.

Suddenly the lights blinked out, and the auditorium was lit only by flames. For a few moments the old Browning Theater lay silent and still. Then the emergency lights flicked on. Once more, trapped fans began screaming and pushing toward the exits.

Frank let out a long sigh of relief. "The generators are off," he said. "Let's get Julie some help." Gently he and Joe carried her off the stage. As they left, they spotted Kaspar and Sullivan running with fire extinguishers to battle the blaze in the seating area.

Joe and Frank took Julie into the dressing room and laid her down on the couch. Within moments her eyes flickered open, though she still didn't look fully conscious.

Phil dashed in from backstage. "Is Julie okay?" he asked.

"We think she's just stunned," Joe replied.

"I couldn't get near the lightning towers, so I had to cut the power at the main breaker," Phil said. "I called the fire department. They're sending an ambulance."

"I'm okay," Julie said. She tried to sit up, but quickly slumped back onto the couch. "I need to get back onstage."

"Show's over," said Ms. Greenberg, standing in the dressing room doorway. "No way the fire department will let us continue tonight. We'll be lucky if they ever let us play in this theater again. Are you sure you're all right, Julie?"

"I'm fine, really." She struggled and sat up. "I just got a little shock, is all."

"We'll let the paramedics determine how well you are," Ms. Greenberg said. "We don't need any band members ending up in the hospital. We've had enough trouble lately. We'll be really lucky if no one sues us over this."

"Yeah," said Ken. He came into the dressing room along with Ray. Both looked at Julie with concern. "I don't know how many more 'accidents' I can take," Ken said.

"Why'd the lightning show go berserk?" Ray asked.

Jackie came in right behind the other two. "I just gave the generators a once-over," she said. "It looks like someone goosed up the power and cut the safety circuits." When Frank looked questioningly at her, she added, "I did all the band's electrical work before we got all these gigs."

"Those generators were fine," Phil said. "I checked them both before the first show. They worked perfectly then."

Ms. Greenberg and the band grew suddenly quiet. "That's right." Ken said, "You *were* in charge of those, weren't you, Cohen?"

"And you were the one who found the cut bungees . . ." Ray noted.

"Don't be silly," Julie said blearily. "Phil's our number-one fan." She shot angry looks at her fellow band members.

"We can vouch for Phil," Frank said. "He's as upstanding as they come."

"And who's going to vouch for you guys?" Ken asked suspiciously. "Just because your dad's some famous detective . . ."

"Maybe you should take a break for a couple of days, Phil," Ms. Greenberg said. "Let the band do some of these upcoming gigs on their own."

"Sure," Phil said, trying not to look hurt. "If that's what everybody wants."

"Well, it's not what *I* want," Julie said angrily. "Phil's done a lot for this band, and he hasn't asked a dime for any of the work he's done. If he goes, I go."

"Julie," Ms. Greenberg said, "this is a really important time for Vette Smash. We can't afford anything more going wrong. You want to land either Miyazaki or Crown as our agent, don't you?"

"Right now," Julie said, "I'm not sure that I care. If we've got to step on our friends to reach the top, maybe I'd rather not get there."

Ken threw his hands up into the air. "This is seriously messed up," he said. "If people are quitting the band tonight, maybe I should start. I'll go solo. What do you think, Billie? Can I make it on my own?"

"As what?" Ray asked. "The Amazing Ego?"

"Cool it, you two," Ms. Greenberg said. "No one's quitting. We've just got some troubles that need to be sorted out. If we stick together . . ."

"Then the lawyers will be able to sue us all at once," Jackie interjected.

"We should go on the lam before the suits start circling," Ken said. "They're probably on their way already. I'm going to go unwind. Who's coming with me?"

"You shouldn't leave the theater before the cops show up," Frank said.

"You can give them my forwarding address," Ken replied. He, Jackie, and Ray headed for the door. Julie looked from her band mates to Phil, but didn't leave the couch.

Ken called back to her. "Hey, Julie. We're going to catch some eats. Meet us at Vince's later—when you get tired of the sharks."

"Sure thing," she replied, speaking through clenched teeth.

"I'll try to intercept the police," Ms. Greenberg said, "and give you a moment to recover."

"Thanks," Julie said.

"Let the paramedics come back here, though," Phil said.

Ms. Greenberg indicated with a nod that she would, then went out front. A few minutes later the dressing room lights clicked on.

"The main power's back," Phil noted.

"The emergency crews must have unplugged the lightning generators and got the rest of the trouble under control," Frank said.

"Now, if only they'd catch the culprit, we could all go home," Joe added.

The paramedics examined Julie for about fifteen minutes before giving her a clean bill of health. They advised her to avoid stress for the next day or two.

Julie chuckled and rolled her eyes. "Sure. No problem."

The police arrived immediately afterward. Gus Sullivan, the father of the band's bouncer, was among the squad. His questioning of Julie, the Hardys, and Phil was brief and routine. He wasn't pleased that the rest of the band had left the scene, but—with his son on the payroll—he seemed convinced he could track them down later.

"We got lucky," Frank said after he had left. "Sullivan's usually a real hard case."

"He probably doesn't want to mess up his son's job," Julie said. "We're trying to take our whole crew to the top with us." She took Phil's hand. "And that includes you too, Phil—no matter what Billie said."

"Hey, I'm just a fan," Phil replied.

"Well, without your help, we wouldn't be where we are today," Julie said.

"Sitting on a ratty couch recovering from electrical shock?" Phil asked, half seriously.

Julie and the Hardys laughed.

"Don't worry, Phil," Frank said. "If the police don't sort this out, Joe and I will."

"We saw Grodd Green and his manager, Dick

71

Devlin, in the audience earlier," Phil said. "Do you think they could have snuck backstage and sabotaged the equipment between sets?"

"It's possible," Frank said. "They definitely have motive, and the theater was pretty chaotic after the first show."

"Let the cops track them down," Julie said. "That's what they're paid for. We can take the rest of the night off and meet the band at Vince's."

"Who's Vince?" Joe asked.

"Not who—*what*," Phil said. "Vince's Powerbar—it's a hot new nightspot down by the river."

"Is that the club that used to be a gym?" Frank asked. "I think I read about it in the paper."

"That's the place," Julie said. "It's the hippest of the hip."

"You're sure you're up to it?" Phil asked.

"You bet," Julie said. Phil helped her from the couch, and they all headed for the back exit. They gave Ms. Greenberg the thumbs-up as she dealt with the police, the fire department, and theater management.

"Sometimes I don't think we pay her enough," Julie said.

Joe nodded. "Tonight you definitely don't."

The four of them piled into the van, and Frank took the wheel.

"Any chance we could catch a bite before hitting

the club?" Joe asked. "After all the excitement, I'm starving."

"Ken usually grabs some fried seafood from the Kool Kone drive-in after a show," Julie said. "If we catch up with the band there, I could apologize for flying off the handle."

"I don't think you owe them any apologies," Joe said. "You were just sticking up for Phil."

"Yeah," Julie replied, "but I still need to work with Vette Smash tomorrow. We don't want the band breaking up over some silly argument—not when we're on the verge of making it big."

"Kool Kone it is, then," Frank said. He pulled the van onto Novick Avenue and headed toward the riverfront.

As they approached the old-style drive-in restaurant, they spotted Ken's red car leaving the parking lot. Ray's restored T-Bird and Jackie's vintage van followed him out.

"Rats! Missed them," Julie said.

"Do you still want to stop for food?" Phil asked.

"Let's grab something at Vince's," Julie said. "It'll be more expensive, but I'd rather get this apology out before I lose my nerve. Could you follow them, Frank?"

"No problem," Frank said. He angled the van to fall into line behind the Vette Smash cars. Before he could pull out, though, a gray, late-model sedan cut him off. Frank hit the brakes hard, barely avoiding a collision.

"Hey!" Joe shouted at the sedan. "Learn to drive!" The sedan's tinted windows were up, though, and he couldn't tell if the driver heard him.

"Hey, calm down," Frank said to his brother. "We know where the band's going. We'll catch up with them at Vince's." He hung back in the traffic, keeping Ken's car in sight. The sedan ahead of them changed lanes frequently. Several times the gray car could have passed Vette Smash's small convoy, but each time an opportunity arose, the sedan ducked back into traffic.

Frank's eyes narrowed. "I think that gray car is following Ken and the others," he said.

"Really?" Julie asked, craning her neck to get a good look at the sedan. "Some of our fans like to hang out with the band, but it's not a car I recognize."

"Maybe it's a new convert, or an autograph seeker," Phil suggested.

"The car's a rental," Joe said, noting the license plates. "Anyone could be driving it."

"Maybe it's a reporter," Julie said. "We've had trouble shaking them lately."

"They almost always use well-marked company cars or vans," Joe said. "But there's another possibility. . . ."

Frank nodded grimly. "Maybe we've found the guy behind the band's troubles."

8 Stalker in the Dark

"Following a band around isn't proof of criminal intent," Phil said.

"It's not," Frank replied, "but you have to know the band's location before you can cause trouble for them. Until now the incidents have taken place at well-publicized events. After the problem with the lightning generators, though, I'd rather err on the side of caution. If someone's following the band, we should keep an eye on him or her. Tailing Vette Smash isn't illegal, but it *is* suspicious."

"It wouldn't be the first time fans have caused trouble for their idols," Joe said. "Some people will do anything just to share the spotlight."

"Since there are rental plates on the car, maybe he's from out of town?" Phil suggested.

"Could be," Frank said. "Though it might be a local who doesn't want his own car identified either—maybe a member of a rival band. Joe, jot down the plate number. Maybe one of our police contacts can track down who rented the car later."

"I'm on it," Joe said. He pulled a pad and pencil from the glove compartment and wrote down the license number. "You know, we could be over-reacting here."

"Better safe than sorry," Frank said.

Vince's Powerbar was a tall brick building near the riverfront. Forty years ago it had been a swanky members-only gym. It had fallen into disrepair during the intervening decades, though—and had become something of an eyesore along the waterway. Last year the Bayport City Council had talked about tearing the old building down. Then celebrity trainer Vince Halter had bought the place and renovated it into a popular nightspot.

The club featured a huge dance floor, blaring techno music, and a health food–oriented grill and bar. Energy drinks were the beverage of choice; no alcohol was allowed on the premises. Because of this, people of all ages mingled in the deafening, strobe-lit darkness.

Cars were jamming the huge parking lot in front of Vince's when the Hardys and their friends pulled in.

"It looks like all of Bayport's here tonight," Joe said.

Ken, Ray, and Jackie pulled up to the front entrance and used the valet parking service for their cars. The gray sedan peeled away and quickly took a handicapped spot near a side entrance.

"He doesn't have a disabled sticker," Phil said.

"Maybe he's counting on leaving before he gets towed," Frank said.

The light near the side entrance was dim, and the car's driver darted inside before they could identify him.

"Joe, I'm going to drop you, Phil, and Julie off," Frank said. He pulled the van up to the entrance the stalker had gone through. "Try to follow him. I'll join you as soon as I find a parking spot."

"Roger that," Joe said, hopping out. He, Phil, and Julie followed their quarry through the side door.

Patrons, dancers, and members of the club's staff jammed Vince's Powerbar—filling it nearly wall-to-wall. The waiters had to hold their trays above their heads as they pushed through the crowd. The lighting in the place was almost nonexistent, except for light from flashing strobes onstage. There was no live music tonight, just a DJ spinning techno discs. The whole room shook with the booming bassline.

Joe peered into the semidarkness and spotted a figure pushing through the crowd in front of them.

"That's him—I think," Joe said, practically shouting to make himself heard above the music. "Flank out. Maybe we can get a look at who it is."

"Good idea," Phil said. "We can come at him from two sides."

"Three," Julie corrected.

Phil shot her a concerned look. "You're sure you're up to it?"

"Positive."

"Well, be careful."

Phil, Julie, and Joe split up, trying to flank the stalker on all sides. Julie went left, Phil right, and Joe bulled his way through the middle.

In the strobe lights everyone seemed to move in slow motion. The illusion didn't help Joe catch his quarry, though. Every time the younger Hardy thought he was getting close, a patron would step out of the darkness and cut him off. Twice he nearly knocked over tray-carrying waiters.

Joe quickly lost track of his friends' exact locations. Occasionally he caught a glimpse of Julie's blond head or Phil's tall, thin form through the crowd. Mostly the two of them remained hidden in the writhing mass of dancers.

The constant thrum of the music made it nearly impossible to hear or even to think. Joe wished he'd come to the club just to dance, rather than to work on a case.

Ordinary objects looked threatening in the flickering darkness. Several times Joe thought he saw a knife in someone's hand. The next strobe flash always revealed the object to be something innocent, though—a pen, a straw, or a cell phone distorted by the lights and the movement of the throng.

Joe pushed ahead as quickly as he could, fighting through the crowd. The dark shape of the stalker loomed just a few yards away now. Joe smiled. In moments he'd catch the man and discover his identity.

Suddenly the lights went out and the music stopped. The crowd cheered and applauded, filling the darkness with deafening sounds. When the strobes flashed on moments later, the stalker had vanished.

Joe looked around, but it was no use. His quarry had slipped away during the brief blackout. The younger Hardy was still kicking himself when Phil intercepted him.

"Any luck?" Phil asked.

Joe shook his head. "I lost him when the lights went out."

"Me too," Phil said. "Let's find Julie."

Bulling through the crowd together, they quickly found the blonde bass player.

"Sorry, guys," Julie said. "He gave me the slip too."

Joe sighed. "There's nothing we can do about it," he said. "Let's head back and find Frank."

The three of them reached the side entrance just as Frank came in. "I thought I'd never find parking," he complained. "I hope you did better with your job."

"Nope," Joe said. "We lost him."

"He looked like a big guy from what I saw," Julie said. "It might have been Grodd Green or Dick Devlin."

"Or maybe Walker Crown," Joe said. "That would make sense with the rental plates. He and Miyazaki are both from out of town."

"Miyazaki could have hired someone to follow the band too, even if it wasn't her," Frank noted. "Big-time agents don't need to do all their own leg work."

"So you think Miyazaki and Crown are keeping tabs on the band?" Phil asked.

"It's possible," Joe said. "An agent wouldn't want to invest a lot of time and money in an act without knowing a lot about it."

"You mean private detectives might be following us around?" Julie said. She shivered. "That gives me the creeps!"

"Your bandmates had better be on their best behavior," Frank said.

"Tell that to Ken," Julie replied with a laugh. "He's behaved badly since birth."

"Did any of you spot the other band members while we were trying to tail that stalker?" Joe asked.

Phil and Julie both shook their heads. "They're probably between the DJ and the dance floor," Julie said. "Ken likes things loud."

"Once we locate them," Frank said, "you should

hang out with the band, Julie. Phil, Joe, and I will make another sweep of the crowd. If we don't turn up anyone suspicious, we'll join you."

"Sounds like a plan," Julie responded.

She guided them across the crowded floor toward the stage. They found Ken, Jackie, and Ray at a table in front of the big loudspeakers. Julie smiled and sat with her friends while Frank, Joe, and Phil melted into the crowd.

"I've got a thought," Joe said. "Let's stake out that gray car. Whoever's driving it has to leave sooner or later. We'll wait in the parking lot and spot them when they go."

"It could be a long wait," Frank said.

"And we don't know for sure that the guy has actually done anything," Phil added.

"That's true," Joe said, "but do either of you have a better idea?"

"We could alert the management that the car's parked illegally," Frank said, "then see who turns up when the tow truck comes."

"That'd move things along, all right," Joe said, smiling at his older brother. "Good plan. I'm on it. You and Phil sweep the crowd again."

"We'll meet you back here," Frank said.

Joe nodded. "I'll call you on Phil's cell phone if I catch the guy."

Twenty minutes later Joe hooked up with Frank and Phil again. "The car split," he reported glumly.

"It was gone before I got a chance to try the plan."

"We didn't spot anyone either," Frank said, frustration in his voice. "This whole tail job has been a complete washout."

"At least the band is safe," Phil said. "For the time being, anyway. Come on, let's call it a night and relax."

They joined Vette Smash at the table near the speakers. The blaring techno music made conversation nearly impossible, but the Hardys gathered that Julie and the others had reconciled. Ken bought them all power shakes, and the group spent the next hour dancing and listening to the music.

During a switch in DJs, Jackie said, "I'm beat." She winked. "That's a drummer joke. Let's head home. We've got another big day tomorrow."

"I'd almost forgotten," Julie said. "We've got that amphitheater fundraiser, don't we?"

"Yeah," Ray said, "the charity concert. Green Machine's on the ticket too, so we'd better be on our toes."

"We'll blow them out of the water," Ken said. "There's no way they can compete with us head-to-head. Julie, do you want a lift back to the apartments?"

"Thanks, Ken," she replied, "but I think I'll ride with Phil." She looked hopefully at her boyfriend and the Hardys. "Assuming you guys want to give me a lift."

"Happy to," Joe said. "As soon as my ears stop ringing."

"We'll meet you at the apartments, then," Ray said.

All of them headed for the parking lot. Ken and the others picked up their cars from the valet service, while Frank rescued the van from the far end of the lot.

"So, the whole band lives in the same apartment?" Joe asked Julie.

She nodded. "In the same complex," she said, "but not the same unit. It makes setting up practices easier—though it also makes it tricky to have any privacy."

"Which way to your place?" Frank asked from behind the wheel.

"It's the old Hotel Claire, on Racine Street," Julie replied.

"A couple of blocks from the courthouse," Frank said. "I know it."

"Ken'll probably beat us there," Julie said. "He drives real fast."

"With a car like his, I'm not surprised," Joe commented.

"Let's hope that Vette Smash doesn't become a prophecy as well as a band name," Phil said.

It took them ten minutes to cross the river, cut through town, and arrive at the apartments. The Hotel Claire had been a boardinghouse in the early part of the twentieth century, before it was converted into an apartment complex thirty years ago. It was a stately brick structure, about four stories high, and it was nestled in an upscale neighborhood. Tall trees lined the street leading past the building, and there was a public park a block farther down.

As they approached the apartments the Hardys and their friends noticed a large group of people standing outside.

"What's going on?" Phil asked.

"I don't know," Julie said. "A block party, maybe?"

"It's a little late in the evening for that," Frank noted.

Julie shrugged. "I really don't care what it is," she said. "I just want to get to bed. You can drop me off by the curb. I'll walk the rest of the way."

Frank pulled over to the side of the road and they all got out. The older Hardy frowned. "I don't like the look of that mob," he said.

A horn beeped, and Ken flashed by in his car. He had the convertible top down and waved as he zipped past, heading for the apartment's tree-lined parking lot. He signaled to make the turn, then stopped, waiting for the crowd to part in front of him.

"There's one of them!" a man cried, pointing at Ken. "Get him!"

9 Mob Rule

The crowd surged forward and pulled Ken out of the open top of his convertible.

"Hey! What are you doing?" Ken cried. "Let go!"

"Come on!" Frank said, dashing to Ken's aid. Joe, Phil, and Julie followed right behind.

Ken had given up on resisting the mob, and was now trying to protect his car. "Watch the paint job!" he yelled. "I just had the detailing redone!" People grabbed at him, yanking his clothes and pulling him in several different directions at once.

"Let go of him!" Joe shouted. He pushed his way through the crowd toward the embattled singer.

The people gathered outside the hotel noticed the Hardys and their friends for the first time. Like a pack of wild animals, the mob turned in one piece. "She's one too," a woman cried, pointing at Julie.

"You owe us restitution!" someone yelled as the mob surged around the four surprised teens.

A moment later Jackie and Ray came down the street and spotted the conflict. Leaving their cars in the middle of the road, they dove into the mob to help their friends.

Everywhere, people were grabbing and pushing. They didn't seem interested in actually hurting the band members, but they were definitely hostile. "What's going on? Why are you doing this?" Julie screamed.

"I nearly got killed at that theater tonight!" one man yelled angrily.

"Give us our money back, you thieves!" bellowed another. "We know you've got it!"

"What are you talking about?" Frank shouted. "No one here has your money!"

Jackie and Ray pushed up beside Frank, forming a tight knot with the Hardys and their friends. Ken was still a short distance away, but the group was moving steadily in his direction. Fear flashed across the faces of the band members.

"Stay together!" Joe called to his friends. "Protect one anothers' backs!"

The crowd came at them again, shoving, grabbing, and screaming accusations.

"They stopped the show and split!" a burly teen

accused, snarling. "With *our* admission money. I heard it on the radio! We came to hear a concert—not to get ripped off!" He aimed a punch at the back of Phil's head.

Joe blocked the blow and elbowed the teen in the side of the head. The angry teen reeled back into the mob, and the crowd surged forward to replace him with someone else. More enraged kids tried to attack them, but Frank kept them back with a series of sweeping martial arts kicks.

"Chill out," the older Hardy said. "You heard wrong. No one here has your money!"

Ken pushed through the crowd and staggered into the small clearing around the Hardys. He looked battered—his clothes were torn. "You want your money back," Ken said to the mob, "talk to the theater. We don't have it!"

The angry fans growled their disbelief. "Liar!" someone called from the back of the group. The crowd surged at the band again.

"Phil, call the cops," Joe said over his shoulder. He blocked a punch aimed at Ray's back.

"Already on it," Phil replied. "I'm calling Billie Greenberg, too. Maybe she can make sense out of this mess."

The crowd milled around them, and one of the people occasionally would try to grab or punch someone in the band. Frank and Joe managed to counter every attack, but grew tired. "We can't hold them off much longer," Frank whispered. "If they all come at us at once . . . there are just too many of them."

A bottle sailed out of the darkness and shattered amid the beleaguered friends. Shards of glass flew through the air, cutting Jackie's cheek and Joe's biceps.

"That's it!" Jackie snarled. She tried to dive into the crowd, but Ray grabbed her T-shirt and held her back. "You'll only make things worse," he hissed.

"I don't think it can get much worse," Ken said. Another bottle flew at them, and another.

Suddenly a siren wailed and red-and-blue lights flashed all around. "This is the police," a deep voice announced on a bullhorn. "Everyone disperse!"

The crowd paused as the Hardys and their friends shook loose from those holding them.

"Step away from the people in the center of the group," the police said. "Anyone not complying will be arrested."

The mob parted as eight uniformed officers surged into view. Through the gap in the crowd, the Hardys spotted a half-dozen patrol cars circling the area. The cops quickly separated the angry swarm from the band members and their friends.

"Good thing the courthouse and police station are so close by," Joe said. He wiped the sweat from his forehead and rubbed his injured arm.

"We're not going home until we've got our

money!" someone shouted from the back of the crowd. The rest grumbled their agreement, refusing to budge.

"But we don't have your money!" Julie said, frustrated.

Officer Sullivan was leading the patrolmen. "What's all this about?" he asked.

Everyone in the crowd started to answer at once. "I can explain, officer," Ms. Greenberg said, her voice cutting above the crowd. She'd parked beyond the police blockade and had run to where the standoff was taking place.

"People got hurt at that concert!" someone shouted.

"I want my money back!" added another.

"It's *them* you should arrest," said a third, pointing to the band.

"Everybody will get their money back," Ms. Greenberg said nervously. "There was a dispute with the theater management and the insurance companies, but it's all worked out now. Everyone holding a valid ticket stub will get a refund. We're covering incident-related medical expenses too."

"What about this?" Ken said angrily, pointing at a broken headlight on his car. "Who's going to pay for that?"

"Did you see who did it?" Sullivan asked.

Ken snarled something unintelligible and shook his head.

"Someone called a local radio program and suggested that Vette Smash had the concert money," Ms. Greenberg explained. "That's what caused people to storm the band's apartment complex."

"Does the radio station know who made the call?" Frank asked.

Ms. Greenberg shook her head. "At this time of night they don't prescreen calls the way they do during the day."

"The police will sort out who's at the bottom of all this," Sullivan said. "Everyone go home and be glad I don't arrest the lot of you for disorderly conduct."

"The local news will carry details on ticket refunds," Ms. Greenberg added.

Sullivan and the other police officers dispersed the crowd. Few in the mob seemed pleased with the resolution, though.

"Come on," Ray said, "let's get our cars off the street and hit the sheets."

"I'm down with that," Jackie said. "This has been one l-o-o-n-g day."

She, Ken, and Ray moved their vehicles into the apartment lot.

"Thanks for taking me home," Julie said to Phil and the Hardys. "I'm glad I didn't walk into this mess alone."

"Happy to help," Phil replied. "See you tomorrow." He and Julie gave each other a quick hug, then the Hardys and Phil got back into the van.

"So," Joe said as they drove home, "who do you think called the radio station and started this mess?"

"Someone wanting to get the band in trouble?" Phil suggested.

"Vette Smash will be all over the local media tomorrow," Frank said. "Some people might think that's a *good* thing."

Joe shook his head. "We've still got a boatload of suspects."

"More than enough to sleep on," Frank replied.

The brothers slept neither long nor well that night. Their alarms woke them for school early the next morning, and they went through the school day like zombies. Only at the end of classes did they start to feel alert.

"I heard on the radio that the police couldn't find out who made that call," Callie said.

"The radio station apologized for running the call unscreened, but denied any responsibility for almost starting a riot," Iola added.

"On the bright side," Phil said, "Vette Smash made it to the top of the local news this morning."

"I bet Walker Crown is happy about that," Joe said. "This stuff could give the band a quick boost into the national spotlight."

"That's a rough road to take, though," Frank said.

"And it seems to me that Green Machine is making out almost as well—but nobody's blaming them for theater disasters or riots in the streets."

"Yeah," Phil said. "The local papers were quoting Dick Devlin a lot. Devlin said his band doesn't attract the kind of troublemakers that Vette Smash does."

Callie sighed. "Vette Smash is winning and losing at the same time."

"I hope today's benefit show can turn things around," Phil said. "Since Green Machine will be playing too, people can compare both bands head-to-head. Speaking of the benefit, I need to get going and help the band set up."

"I thought Greenberg didn't want you helping," Joe said.

"She called this morning and apologized for that," Phil replied. "I think Julie and the band pushed her into it. Are you girls coming along?"

Callie and Iola shook their heads. "Thanks, Phil," Callie said, "but Iola and I are hoping to stay out of the spotlight for a while."

"We're going up to the farm for the weekend," Iola added. "You know us—all work and no play."

"Say hello to Chet for us when you see him," Joe said. He gave Iola a quick hug.

"I will," she replied. "You two stay safe."

"Always," Frank said, giving Callie a hug as well.

The girls headed off to the farm, while Frank and Joe gave Phil a lift in the van. "So, where's the gig today?" Joe asked as he pulled the van out of the school parking lot.

"The Riverside Amphitheater," Phil replied. "The concert is going to feature a lot of local bands."

"Including Vette Smash's biggest rivals," Frank noted.

"Yeah," Phil said. "It's a pretty cool setup. All the bands will be playing the same instruments. After the concert's over, the instruments are being auctioned off for charity."

"Sounds like a good way to raise money," Joe said. "Fans of all the bands will be bidding against one another."

"Right. In this case, the band rivalries may work to everyone's advantage," Frank said.

"I hope that means the other bands will be on their best behavior," Phil said. "We could use a quiet night."

"I wouldn't count on it," Joe said.

The Riverside Amphitheater was open to the air in front, but it still had traditional backstage and underground areas for readying performances. The theater's dressing rooms were larger and better appointed than the ones at the Browning. The amphitheater had plenty of space to accommodate the competing bands, since it had been built for classical concerts featuring full orchestras.

Phil's pass got the Hardys a spot in the underground parking lot, which connected directly to the backstage area. As they exited the garage elevator, the three friends ran right into Grodd Green and his crew.

"Well, if it ain't the Vette Smash hangers-on," Green said. "Let us know when you feel like following a *real* band."

"Hmm. Know any?" Joe asked.

The leader of the Green Machine looked as though he might punch Joe, but Dick Devlin stepped in between the two. "Now, now," Devlin said to his star performer, "save the fire for the performance." Then to the Hardys and Phil, he added, "You three scram before I call security." Phil and the brothers just laughed and walked away.

On their way to the dressing rooms, Phil, Frank, and Joe passed both Walker Crown and Kelly Miyazaki. Crown waved hello; Miyazaki didn't even notice them.

A series of buffet tables sat to one side of the backstage area. The Hardys spotted Ms. Greenberg and Vette Smash working their way through the amphitheater staff toward the food. Ken and the band paused long enough to sign some autographs on their way.

"Hey," Phil called to Ms. Greenberg, "what do you need me to do?"

"Thanks for coming, Phil," she replied, "but it looks like we don't need your help after all. The venue crew is setting up. We're practically ready to go. But I'm glad you're here—I want to apologize again for what I said yesterday. The band really needs supporters like you. Grab yourselves some food and relax. I need to go talk to Crown and Miyazaki before the show." She bustled off, leaving the group waiting near the buffet.

A half-dozen folding tables had been set up to accommodate the food, though the ones nearest the Hardys were empty. Vette Smash, their crew members, and some people from other bands were digging into the refreshments on the other tables.

"Should we wait, or get in line now?" Frank asked. He leaned on one of the empty tables, and his foot kicked something on the floor. The object skidded out from under the table and came to a stop against Joe's shoe.

Joe picked up the small glass bottle and examined it.

Affixed to the bottle was a bright yellow label marked POISON.

10 Bad Eats

Joe looked from the empty bottle to the crowd gathered around the refreshment table. The members of Vette Smash and a number of other bands moved around the buffet, dishing food onto plastic plates. They laughed and chatted amiably with one another, unaware of the danger.

"Stop!" Joe cried.

"Don't eat that food!" Frank shouted.

The Hardys ran toward the main buffet table. Most of the people gathered around the table looked at the brothers as though they were crazy.

"That food may have been poisoned," Joe said, holding up the empty bottle of rat poison.

Some people dropped their plates. Others quickly backed away from the table. The members of Vette Smash eyed their food as though it might bite them. Geo Kaspar froze in midchew, a big mouthful of dip in his mouth. He swallowed hard, then glanced around nervously.

"We found this bottle on the floor," Frank said, indicating the spot near the empty table. As everyone looked, a caterer came out and put a new platter of food down where, moments before, the Hardys had discovered the poison.

"So what?" Ken said, trying to sound unperturbed. "It's rat poison. Theaters have rats sometimes. Maybe someone was cleaning up before the show and got careless."

"Do you really want to take that chance?" Joe asked.

Ken put down his plate. "All right—not me," he said. "I've had enough excitement lately." The rest of Vette Smash dropped their food on the table as well. Members of the other bands and their crews did the same.

"This stinks," someone exclaimed. "Big time! We need eats before the show."

"The food that guy just brought in *can't* be poisoned," Jackie pointed out. "Not unless the chef did it."

The caterer bringing in the new food looked puzzled. "I assure you," he said, "all of our food is of the highest quality." He turned in a huff and walked away to get another platter. Jackie and the rest grabbed for the buffet he'd just laid out.

Kaspar stood to one side of the group, slowly turning green.

"Are you okay?" Julie asked.

Kaspar shook his head, put his hand over his mouth, and ran for the backstage restrooms.

Joe and Frank followed him in. "I'll call an ambulance," Frank offered.

"No!" Kaspar blurted from inside a stall. "I'm okay, really. Just a bit of stomach upset."

"But it might be poison," Joe said.

"Don't worry about it," Kaspar said stubbornly. "I can handle it. The band doesn't need any more bad publicity."

"Well, if you're not out in a couple of minutes, we're calling the paramedics," Frank said.

"Suit yourself," Kaspar replied. "I don't need 'em."

"Is Geo okay?" Julie asked as the Hardys left the restroom.

"He says he is, but . . ." Joe shrugged. "He's being pretty stubborn. He won't let us call anyone."

"Do you think he ate some of the poison?" Phil asked.

"Who can tell?" Frank replied. "We'll give him a few minutes and see if he feels better."

Ms. Greenberg had returned from her errand and, after hearing the news, was looking nervously around the buffet area. "Maybe Geo's trouble is psychosomatic," she suggested upon hearing the

Hardys. "You find an empty poison bottle, so he thinks he must have eaten some."

"I never noticed Geo having a weak stomach before," Phil said.

"The police will have to investigate in any case," Frank said. "Trying to poison someone is a serious offense."

"We'll handle this, if you don't mind," said a dapper-looking man in a tuxedo.

"This is Mr. Copeland," Ms. Greenberg said. "He runs the amphitheater."

"I'll have the officers on the scene look into this problem," Copeland said. His tone made it clear that he thought the Hardys and their friends might have been exaggerating the trouble. "My staff will make sure Mr. Kaspar is tended to as well. You needn't concern yourselves further. Everything is under control."

"But—," Joe began.

"We put on many events here," Copeland said, cutting him off. "We've seen all manner of crises. I assure you, everything will be taken care of, and it will all be done by the book. All you need do is make yourselves available to the police, should they want to question you."

"That's no problem," Ms. Greenberg said brightly.

Copeland held out his hand to Joe. "I'll take that bottle, if you don't mind," he said. Reluctantly Joe handed it to him. Copeland flashed Joe a false smile, then motioned for the amphitheater staff to clear away the tables of questionable food. "See," he said, "the show continues with no untidy interruptions." He gave a curt bow and vanished into the wings once more.

Frank gritted his teeth. "Yes," he said, "no untidy investigations of a possible crime scene."

"I'd think you boys would be glad to be out of the middle of this," Ms. Greenberg said. "Let Copeland's staff handle it. And please keep out of the way during the performance?" She smiled insincerely, then left as well.

"Boy," Joe fumed, "the way she's talking, you'd think *we* poisoned that food."

"She's had a bad couple of days," Julie said. "We all have. If it makes you feel better, *I* don't think you're behind this trouble any more than Phil is."

"Thanks, Julie," Phil said. "I just wish we could catch a break from these minidisasters."

"We won't catch a break until we've caught the one causing these problems," Frank said.

"Let's grab some of the unpoisoned food," Joe said. "I can't think on an empty stomach."

They joined the crowd around the newly set buffet tables and dug in. A few minutes later Kaspar, still looking a bit green, returned from the restroom. He gave the members of Vette Smash a weak smile and a thumbs-up, then tottered toward the dressing rooms to rest.

Todd "Grodd" Green and the members of Green Machine arrived as Kaspar left. They laughed as the big man staggered away. "No wonder you Vette Smash guys are having trouble," Green said, "if that's the quality of your road crew!"

"Ignore him," Ray said. "He just craves attention."

"Speaking of attention," Green said, "what was all this noise? Another Vette Smash publicity stunt gone bad? You guys know you can't beat us onstage, so you've got to steal the media spotlight any way you can."

"Dream on, Todd," Jackie said.

"It'd be just your style to poison that food to put us out of action, Green," Ken said. "You know that guitar-to-guitar, you can't win."

Ken and Green glared at each other and stepped away from the table. Before they could start fighting, though, Crown and Miyazaki appeared from the wings and stepped between them.

"My, but if this don't look like an old-fashioned Texas donnybrook in the making," Crown said. "Pardon my interfering, boys, but shouldn't you be using those hands for playing guitar rather than for punching each other out?"

"A broken hand wouldn't hurt Todd's playing any," Ken said.

"And it might improve Fender's," Green shot back.

"Now that's what I like," Crown said, putting his arms around both band leaders' shoulders. "Feisty. Feisty is good in a rock band. I can use that."

"Assuming, of course, that any of them hire you," Ms. Miyazaki said. "Is there anything that *isn't* a promotion to you, Walker?"

"Nope," Crown replied with a grin. "I see everything as an opportunity. That's the difference between us, Kelly."

"That's the difference between Ms. Greenberg and me too," said a new voice. Dick Devlin appeared from the dressing room area. He was dressed to the nines in a black suit with a gold tiepin and matching cufflinks. "You Vette Smash people ought to drop Billie and hook up with me. There's plenty of room in my stable for two great bands."

"But if we signed with you, you'd still only have one," Jackie quipped.

"And some of us like to wake up every morning without having to count our fingers to make sure none are missing," Ray added.

Devlin sighed, shook his head, and shrugged. "I don't know what you and Miyazaki see in these punks, Crown. I extend my hand in friendship, and they try to bite it off."

"It's just youthful high spirit," Crown replied. "That's what I like about *both* bands."

"And I thought we were trying to sign talent, not spirits," Ms. Miyazaki commented.

Crown shot her an ingratiating smile. "Enough repartee. Let's grab some eats before the show starts." He and Miyazaki crowded toward the refreshment table, along with Devlin and the members of the Green Machine. Ken and Vette Smash headed for their dressing rooms, and Phil and the Hardys tagged along.

"Which band is playing first?" Joe asked.

"We don't know yet," Julie said. "It's going to be determined by random draw, just before the concert."

"Devlin and Billie tried to work it out beforehand," Ken said, "but they couldn't agree."

"We didn't want Green Machine going first, and they didn't want us to," Ray explained.

"So it's a draw . . . literally," Jackie finished.

"Give us a few minutes alone to get psyched up, will you guys?" Ken asked, pausing at his dressing room door. "We want Vette Smash to be ready and rearin' to go when they call us onstage."

"No problem," Phil said. "Want me to check over the setup?"

"Nah," Ken said. "Since all the bands are using the same instruments, the amphitheater folks have already done it."

"Won't it be difficult playing on instruments that don't belong to you?" Frank asked.

"Yeah," Julie replied, "but that's part of the challenge. It'll make it that much sweeter when we kick

Green Machine's butt." She blew Phil a kiss, and the band retired to their dressing rooms.

"Boy, is this a hornet's nest," Joe said. "We've got rival agents, rival managers, rival bands—any one of whom could be behind Vette Smash's streak of bad luck."

"Someone in Vette Smash could be behind it too," Frank said.

"You don't mean that!" Phil said, alarmed.

"It's all a matter of whether it's bad luck or good publicity," Joe said. "The band's been on the news a lot in the last few days. So has Ken."

"He seemed serious about going solo," Frank mused.

"Right—and a member of Vette Smash would have the kind of inside knowledge that would make these 'accidents' a cinch to set up," Joe added. "So would Billie Greenberg, for that matter. Maybe she's from the same publicity school Crown hails from."

Phil sat in a folding chair and put his head in his hands. "I just can't believe that any one of them could be responsible for this. People could have been hurt—or worse." He sighed, long and loud. "I guess I'm just too close to the situation."

Joe put his arm around Phil's shoulder. "Fortunately you have me and Frank to help sort things out."

The three of them talked quietly about the case for the next twenty minutes. They went over the incidents and who might have been responsible for them. As the bands came out of their dressing rooms, though, the three seemed no closer to solving the case.

Suddenly Grodd Green stormed past the trio, looking angry. "Well, that *stinks!*" he shouted. "I want a redraw."

Billie Greenberg and the rest of the two bands followed in his wake. "There's no way we're giving up the first spot," Ms. Greenberg said. "You'll just have to play in the middle of the show and like it." She gave Green an insincere smile. "Sorry, Todd."

"You set this up somehow!" Todd said, turning on her. "You've been dying to get your no-talents in the spotlight, and now—thanks to a few 'incidents'— you've got them there. You'll do anything to put your band on top."

Ken stepped between his manager and Green. "As if Dick Devlin wouldn't do the same for you. He might even cut a guy's bungee cord just before a publicity jump. Hmm? Don't think I didn't see you and Devlin at the bridge before I drove off!"

"Cool down, all of you," Dick Devlin said. "The show's about to start."

"I don't have to take that kind of attitude from Fender's talentless cronies," Green said. "Come on Machine—let's go!" He and his fellow band members turned and sprinted toward the stage.

"Hey!" Julie called. "*We're* supposed to be on first!"

But it was too late. The crowd that had already assembled in the amphitheater had spotted Green Machine as the members trotted onstage. Grodd Green thrust his fist into the air, acknowledging the crowd's roar.

"Devlin!" Ms. Greenberg hissed. "You put them up to this!"

Dick Devlin merely laughed.

Green Machine took their places and picked up the instruments. Grodd Green shot a wicked smile toward Vette Smash. Ken and his bandmates stood backstage, flabbergasted.

"Somebody ought to fix that guy good!" Jackie said.

"To the victors go the spoils!" Green bellowed into the microphone.

He thrust his fist into the air once more, and again the crowd roared their approval. The Green Machine drummer began a machine gun–like patter. The rest of the band joined in, building in anticipation of the first huge power chord from Green's electric guitar.

Grodd Green wound up, swung his guitar pick high into the air, and brought it down across the strings.

As he did, sparks flew from the body of the guitar. Green's eyes shot open, and he fell, quaking, to the stage.

11 Shock Rock

Grodd Green twitched on the floor, his body shaking as though he'd been struck by lightning.

The audience screamed. Stunned, the other members of Green Machine stopped in midchord. None of them made a move to help their leader.

Green's hands clenched tightly around the guitar, as though frozen to it. Sparks blazed from the instrument and the wooden body of the guitar caught fire.

Frank and Joe dashed across the stage toward Green. Frank dove at the guitar's cords. He seized them and yanked them out. An electrical popping sound filled the air, and the amplifiers onstage crackled from the sudden disconnection.

Joe pulled the burning guitar out of Green's

hands and tossed it aside. "Green!" Joe said. "Are you okay?"

The leader of Green Machine looked blearily at the younger Hardy. Then Grodd Green's eyes grew cold and angry. "What do you think you're doing?" he asked. He pushed Joe away and tried to stand.

Recovered from their surprise, the other members of the Machine swarmed around Green and helped him to his feet.

"Saving your life, that's what," Joe said. "You might try thanking us." Behind him Frank doused the flaming guitar with a bottle of water he'd found near the drum stand.

"Thank you . . . ?" Green said, incredulous. "For all I know, you guys did this on purpose."

"Hey, you're the one who bullied your way onstage," Joe said.

Green thrust a finger at him. "So *that's* your motive. You and your Vette Smash buddies can't stand the heat. Well, I'm not anybody's fall guy." He turned to the other members of the band. "Come on, Machine, we're out of here!" They all turned and stalked off the stage.

"Good riddance!" Joe called after them.

"Take it easy, Joe," Frank said, putting a hand on his brother's shoulder. "Let's head backstage and try to sort this out." The Hardys left the stage and took the scorched guitar with them. As they went Mr. Copeland entered the stage from the opposite direction and began calming down the crowd.

"What happened out there?" Ms. Greenberg asked the brothers.

"Looks like a short circuit in the guitar," Frank said. He held up the singed instrument.

"It's the worst I've ever seen," said Phil, examining the guitar. He shot the brothers a look that said he doubted the short had been an accident.

"Can it be fixed?" Ms. Greenberg asked.

"I doubt it," Phil replied.

"Maybe Geo could repair it," Ray suggested. "He's a whiz at patching things together before shows."

"I think he's still in the dressing room, recovering," Julie said.

"We should let him rest. . . ." Ms. Greenberg said. "But the show can't continue without a lead guitar to play." She looked worried. "If this concert is canceled, it could really hurt the band."

"Canceling the concert won't do our benefit any good either," Copeland said, joining the conversation. "I've calmed the crowd down, but it'll be at least an hour before I can get another instrument brought in."

"No sweat," Ken said. "My guitar's out in my car. I'll donate it to the cause. That's assuming, of course, that Vette Smash gets to play next—and that we also get to return for an encore at the end of the show."

"Well," Copeland said, "you were supposed to go

on first, anyway—so that's no problem. And we were hoping to get all the artists back for a final encore jam, too."

"I doubt Green Machine will be returning," Jackie said.

Copeland frowned at her, then turned back to Ken. "I guess you have a deal, young man," he said. "Go grab that guitar."

Ken hurried off to the underground parking area to get his instrument.

Ms. Greenberg sighed with relief. "Well . . . that problem's solved. I'll go make sure things are set up for when Ken returns." She bustled off to talk to the amphitheater staff.

"Phil, if you want to look over the stage setup, we'd all appreciate it," Julie said.

"We've had enough shocks for today," Ray added, a slight smile spreading across his face.

"Sure thing," Phil said. He went to check out the amps and other equipment while Vette Smash prepared to take the stage.

Frank pulled Joe into a quiet corner of the backstage area. "Ms. Greenberg was right," Frank said, "that short circuit solved Vette Smash's problem with the Green Machine—at least at this concert."

"I don't see how she could have arranged the accident, though," Joe replied. "Ken could have been playing that guitar just as easily as Green. If Green Machine hadn't stormed the stage . . ."

". . . Ken would be recovering from the shock of his life, and the Machine would be headlining right now," Frank said, finishing his brother's thought. "You're right. That jolt could have been meant for Ken."

"But if the Machine set it up, why'd they fall into their own trap?" Joe wondered. "It seems like a big risk to take for publicity."

"Maybe the guitar was supposed to short out later in the show," Frank suggested. "Maybe that's why Green was in such a rush to perform."

"You'd need a lot of electronic expertise to rig a time-delayed short circuit," Joe said. "I don't know if even Phil could do it. And when'd the saboteur rig the guitar, anyway? Those instruments are only being used for this one show."

"If not for the incidents over the past few days," Frank said, "I'd write this off as an accident."

"Maybe," Joe said.

Ken returned with his guitar in less than ten minutes, and Vette Smash was ready to go. The band stormed the stage, much the way that Green Machine had done earlier. The fans in the amphitheater gave them a thundering ovation as the band ripped into "I Would Dive for You."

"Everything onstage checked out," Phil said to the Hardys as they watched the show from the wings.

"Which means that the lead guitar was the only sabotaged instrument," Frank said.

111

"But who was the target?" Joe mused.

The show didn't answer that question. Vette Smash rocked the house and left the audience standing and screaming for more. The acts that followed were good, but not up to the level of Ken and his band.

Ken, Julie, and the rest of the band returned for a fabulous encore jam, bringing the audience to their feet once more. As the final notes of "Jumpin' Jack Flash" faded into the cool, Bayport evening, the band raced backstage to unwind. Mr. Copeland immediately took center stage to begin the charity auction.

Vette Smash exchanged high fives with Ms. Greenberg, the Hardys, and Phil.

Kaspar, still looking a bit green, sat in a chair nearby and gave them another thumbs-up. "Sorry I didn't catch most of the show," he said, "but the encore really rocked."

"You guys did great," Ms. Greenberg said. "I'm predicting record numbers for the charity auction."

"Hey, I might bid myself," Ken said, "just to get my favorite guitar back." They all laughed.

Walker Crown and Kelly Miyazaki mingled through the throng backstage, glad-handing the other bands before finally making their way to Vette Smash.

"Listen to that crowd," Crown said, cupping an ear toward the amphitheater. "They still want more—

and they'll pay almost any price to get a piece of it."

"Lucky for the Bayport charities," Frank said.

"I've changed my mind," Ms. Miyazaki said, "maybe this series of fiascoes was actually a *brilliant* publicity campaign. I almost wish I'd cooked it up myself." She smiled at the band. "So, when do you sign with me?"

"Hold on there just a minute," Crown said. "Vette Smash is signing with *me*. We practically shook hands on the deal."

"*Practically* doesn't count, Walker," Ms. Miyazaki said, "except in horseshoes and hand grenades. Come down to my hotel suite in the morning, Ms. Greenberg, and we'll sign the papers."

"Billie, darlin'," Crown said, "you know I'll top whatever Miyazaki has to offer."

"Walker, you're all hat and no cattle," Miyazaki countered. "Vette Smash needs an agent who can help them to the top, not one that wants to ride their gravy train."

"My mother always said," Ms. Greenberg said slowly, "that only a fool signs a contract without having a good night's sleep. Both of you can drop your proposals by my office tomorrow morning. The band and I will look them over. . . ."

"And then sign with whoever offers us an island in the Caribbean and their firstborn child," Jackie said.

Crown stuck his hands in his pockets and looked

113

glum. "Well, Billie," he said, "if that's the way you want to play it."

Miyazaki pushed her dark glasses up on her nose. "I'll have the proposal for you first thing in the morning," she said. "Good night, all. Come on, Walker; my future stars need their rest." She turned on her heel and left.

"You mean *my* future stars," Crown said, following her out.

As soon as the agents had gone, Billie Greenberg and the band exchanged high fives again. "We're in!" Julie exclaimed.

"Not yet," Ms. Greenberg cautioned. Then she smiled. "But we're *close*."

Ken frowned. "Like Ms. Miyazaki said, 'practically doesn't count.' I'm not banking my money until my name is on a contract."

"But until then," Ray said, "we should *party!*"

"Well," Ms. Greenberg said, "a small celebration might be in order. Not for me, though—I've got to get some rest if I'm going to sort through those contract proposals tomorrow."

Jackie shook her head at Ms. Greenberg. "All work and no play . . . ," she said, smiling.

"Promise me you'll take it easy tonight," Ms. Greenberg continued. "We don't need any more incidents before we sign."

"Hey, this is my career we're talking about," Ken said. "I'll be careful."

"Our careers, you mean," Julie countered.

Ms. Greenberg smiled at the band. "I know you don't have another gig until late tomorrow night at Vince's, but why don't you all stop by my office around dinnertime. We'll grab something to eat and talk over the proposals then."

"Sounds like a plan," Ray said. "Good night, Billie."

Vette Smash's manager exchanged good-byes with the group, then headed for home. The band members went to their dressing rooms, freshened up, and changed into their street clothes.

Phil and the Hardys hung out backstage until they returned.

"Copeland stopped by," Phil told the band. "The auction set a record—just like Ms. Greenberg predicted."

"After all the media attention, I'm not surprised," Ken said. He smiled, obviously pleased with himself. "Let's grab some Kool Kone and then go dancin' or something."

"Sounds like a plan," Joe said.

The Hardys, Phil, and the band took the backstage elevator to the underground parking facility. They laughed and joked as they rode down, feeling some of the pressure from the last few days finally wearing off.

The elevator doors opened on the bottom level, and they all stepped into the dimly lit garage.

Frank scanned the lot, noting the low level of

light in the huge concrete structure. "Weren't there more lights on earlier?" he asked.

Before Joe could answer, someone jumped them from behind.

12 Battle of the Bands

Frank's head hit the pavement and stars flashed before his eyes. He felt himself being roughly pulled to his feet, but it took a few moments before his vision cleared. In the dim light he could barely discern the smiling face of Grodd Green. Behind Green stood a group of very angry-looking Green Machine fans.

"We thought we'd give you a little payback for what happened onstage," Green said. The mob with him had Vette Smash, Joe, and Phil—as well as Frank—firmly in their clutches.

"You jerk!" Julie hissed. "We didn't have anything to do with that guitar accident!"

"You better let us go," Joe said, "before you get in real trouble." He, like Frank, was being held by two guys in Green's mob. It seemed the Machine had at least two people for every member of Vette Smash's crew.

Grodd Green sneered at Joe. "Who's going to give us that trouble, blondie? You?"

"You bet," Joe said. He pitched forward, flipping one of the guys holding him over his head. He smashed the other in the face with his elbow. He pushed himself free as both thugs went down.

Frank stomped down hard on the foot of one of his captors. The bully yelped and hopped away as Frank judo-flipped his other assailant. Frank's second captor hit the pavement hard and lay still. Frank stepped over him to help free Phil and the rest.

The Hardys' action galvanized the members of Vette Smash. They all began fighting tooth and nail against their ambushers. In seconds the parking garage became a chaotic mess. The two rival band leaders squared off against each other at the center of the action.

Grodd Green swung at Ken. Ken ducked out of the way, but one of Green Machine's fans clouted Vette Smash's leader on the back of the head. Ken went down, but Joe came to his rescue.

The younger Hardy threw a perfect block between the Machine members and their intended victim. Joe knocked the feet out from under Green and his pals. All of the attackers sprawled onto their faces.

Frank batted aside a punch aimed at Phil, then

felled his attacker with a quick chop to the neck. "Take Julie and call the police," Frank said. He pushed Phil away from the melee. Phil then helped Julie escape her assailants, and the two of them ran for the Hardys' van. As he ran Phil fished his cell phone out of his pocket.

A black-shirted Green Machine thug swung a bottle at Jackie. She stepped out of the way, but backed into a concrete pillar. Joe quickly left Grodd Green on the ground and went to rescue Jackie.

Joe grabbed the wrist of the attacker and twisted it so that the bottle flew through the air and smashed harmlessly onto the pavement. Joe slammed his other fist into the black-shirted man's gut. The man staggered back, and Joe pushed him into the advancing throng.

Green's mob fell back, disorganized and stunned by the sudden resistance. The Hardys and their friends were still badly outnumbered, though. The horde gathered its courage and surged forward once more.

Ken kicked Grodd as he tried to get up. Ray took off his leather Vette Smash jacket and swung it around like a whip, keeping the hostile crowd at bay. Jackie belted the Green Machine's drummer in the face. Frank and Joe fought back-to-back, each protecting the other. Slowly but surely, the brothers and Vette Smash worked their way toward the Hardys' van.

Grodd Green wiped a few drops of blood from his mouth and snarled, "Get them!"

Suddenly sirens and flashing red-and-blue lights filled the garage. Police squad cars raced into the parking structure. One pulled up in front of the mob, cutting them off from the elevator. Another blocked the exit ramp, while a third parked in front of the emergency stairwell. Armed policemen poured from the cars and surrounded the crowd.

"This is the police!" an amplified voice boomed. "Everybody freeze!"

Mr. Copeland appeared out of the elevator, a handful of private security guards at his side. He walked directly to the officer in charge and said, "I would appreciate it very much if you would arrest every one of these hooligans."

Completely penned in, the mob surrendered quietly. Frank and Joe sighed with relief.

Copeland eyed the Hardys and their friends coldly. "I told you I could take care of trouble," he said.

The police read the entire crowd their rights, then took everyone to the station downtown. Everyone in the melee was fingerprinted and given their one free phone call. The Hardys and Phil called their parents. The band members called their managers.

At one fifteen Friday night, Fenton and Laura Hardy arrived at the police station with the family

120

lawyer. Phil's parents came with their lawyer too.

An hour and a half later, the lawyers, the managers, and the police had finally sorted everything out. Mr. Hardy and Mrs. Hardy obtained permission to take their sons home. Mrs. Hardy drove the car home, while Mr. Hardy agreed to drive the brothers back in the van.

The famous detective and his sons sat in the station's lobby while they waited for the final paperwork to clear. Phil and Julie had been released as well, and sat on the bench next to the Hardys.

"I'm glad that you two and Phil won't be charged," Mr. Hardy said. "Clearly you were just protecting yourselves. But how did all this happen?" He looked very stern.

"Grodd Green and his buddies were waiting in the garage beneath the amphitheater and jumped us after the concert," Joe replied.

"They knocked out a couple of lights to create an element of surprise," Frank added.

"That'll mean a charge of vandalism to start," Phil said, "along with assault."

"Neither the Green Machine kids nor Vette Smash are going be charged," Mr. Hardy said. "The bands wouldn't press charges against each other."

Frank and Joe looked at each other, puzzled, then at Julie. She blushed and turned away.

"Well, I'm betting that Copeland will press charges," Frank said. "He's got to be ticked off that his facility's garage became the site of a rumble."

"He was angry, but the band managers got together and promised to pay for the damages," Mr. Hardy said. "Copeland doesn't want the bad publicity either. As much as I hate to say it, it looks like no one's getting more than a slap on the wrist for this brawl."

"We're paying fines for disorderly conduct," Julie said. Her voice was quiet, apologetic.

"Hey, it's not your fault Green attacked us," Phil said.

Julie buried her head in her hands. "I just feel like I've dragged you guys into a lot of trouble."

"Believe me," Frank said, "Joe and I have had worse."

Mr. Hardy sighed. "Sad to say, but true. No more trouble tonight, though, if you please."

"No way, Dad," Joe said. "After you drive us home, we're heading right to bed."

"Good thing it's Saturday," Frank said. "I feel like I could sleep for a week."

"Me too," agreed Phil.

"You don't have a week," Julie said. "We need you to help set up the next show." Then, smiling weakly, she added, "But the band doesn't play until midnight."

The Hardys slept until just before noon. They made brunch for their parents to apologize for the late-night trip to the police station, and then did their chores. And as they worked they puzzled over the case.

"Green Machine's at the top of my suspect list now," Joe said. "Though that mob action doesn't explain the guitar that shocked Grodd Green."

Frank shook his head. "If Green had arranged that accident and got caught by mistake, why'd he storm off the stage? He could have been a hero if he'd kept playing despite nearly being killed."

"Maybe that's why he assembled that mob," Joe suggested. "He was mad at himself for blowing it, big time. The only thing left to do was to beat up the competition."

"But Vette Smash really benefited from the sabotaged guitar," Frank said. "Ms. Greenberg is meeting with Crown and Miyazaki even now. The band could have a major contract by the end of the day."

"Which makes everyone in Vette Smash suspect, as well as Ms. Greenberg," Joe said. He ran his fingers through his blond hair and sighed. "The music business is way too cutthroat for me."

Just then the phone rang, and Frank picked it up. "Oh, hey, Phil," Frank said. He motioned for Joe to pick up the other phone.

"With the band playing at midnight, we've got most of the day off," Phil said. "Julie and I were thinking of having a picnic. I've borrowed a pair of motorcycles from my cousin and we were going to drive up along the shore. Julie doesn't drive cycles, so we've got an extra. Want to tag along?"

"Are you sure we wouldn't be in the way?" Frank asked.

"Nah," Phil said. "After the way you defended the band during that melee, taking you on a picnic is the least Julie and I can do."

"We're in, then," Joe said. He and Frank hung up their phones, then drove over to Phil's house to pick up the bikes.

Phil checked to make sure the brothers knew how to handle the equipment, then the three of them motored over to Julie's apartment, with Frank riding with Joe. They parked the motorcycles at the edge of the parking lot, then hiked up to Julie's unit.

Her second-floor walk-up wasn't very large—just a couple of rooms with a kitchenette. It was filled nearly to overflowing with CDs, accessories for her bass guitar, Vette Smash costumes, and music memorabilia. Frank and Joe took a few moments to admire Julie's vintage Jimi Hendrix posters as she finished getting ready.

"I noticed quite a bit of equipment lying around your apartment." Frank said as they headed downstairs. "Do you tinker with guitars much?"

"Only enough to keep my bass running," Julie replied. "Anything more serious, I let the pros handle. Geo's probably the best on the crew, but most of the roadies know their way around the instruments we play. They're paid to handle the equipment."

"As opposed to me," Phil added, shooting her a smile.

"Phil's my favorite indentured servant," she said, smiling back.

They put on their helmets and packed their sandwiches and sodas into the small storage compartments beneath the motorcycle seats. Joe climbed aboard behind Frank, while Julie mounted up behind Phil.

As they pulled to the edge of the lot Julie slapped her hand to her helmet. "Forgot something," she said, climbing down off the back of Phil's bike. "Be right back."

She dashed across the tree-lined parking lot into the building's side entrance. A few minutes later she came out the door and walked back across the lot toward her friends.

As she did the roar of a powerful engine filled the air.

Julie turned as a bright red car pulled out of a secluded space in the back of the parking lot.

She stopped and peered at the car's tinted windows. "Ken?" she asked.

The car was heading straight for her.

13 Vette Dash

"Julie, look out!" Phil yelled.

Julie ran across the pavement toward Phil and the Hardys. The cars parked on either side hemmed her in, giving her little room to maneuver. The sports car continued to barrel forward.

Phil leaped off his bike and ran to help. He yanked her out of the way just as the car was about to hit her. The car brushed the back of Julie's legs and spun her around. She pitched forward, hitting her helmeted head hard on the pavement. Phil stretched out on the concrete beside her.

Frank and Joe dashed up to their friends as the sports car screeched out of the parking lot.

"Phil! Julie!" Frank yelled.

"I'm okay," Phil said, slowly sitting up. Julie was lying still, her eyes closed.

"She's breathing, but . . ." Joe said.

"Don't move her," Frank said. "There's no way to tell how badly she might be hurt."

"I'll call an ambulance," Phil said, pulling out his cell phone. Burning rage filled his eyes. "There's nothing you two can do for Julie," he said, "but you can still catch Ken before he gets away."

"We're on it," Joe said. He and Frank leaped onto the bikes and fired up the engines. They roared out of the parking lot, hot on the tail of the red sports car.

The sports car headed west, away from downtown Bayport. It wound through traffic, causing other cars to swerve out of the way. Frank and Joe kept as close as they could while trying not to endanger any other motorists or pedestrians.

On Tierney Avenue, just east of the interstate, Frank saw a chance to catch up. The road in front of them was straight, and clear of other cars. The older Hardy gunned the bike's accelerator and pulled alongside their quarry.

Frank couldn't see through the convertible's tinted windows, but he signaled the driver to pull over. The sports car swerved left toward Frank's motorcycle.

Frank veered out of the way, nearly crossing over the double yellow line. The tires of his cycle squealed, and he fought hard to keep from skidding out.

The red car cut back to the right, heading down Hebert Boulevard and into the wooded hills on Bayport's outskirts.

Joe pulled up alongside his brother. "You okay?" he called.

Frank nodded. "Let's catch this jerk!" he said, shouting to be heard over the roar of the engines and the whistle of the wind.

They rocketed onto Hebert Boulevard, but Ken had already extended the distance between them. The red car disappeared over the top of the next rise, just as the brothers started uphill.

The Hardys' bikes took to the air as they crested the hill. They landed smoothly and raced into a series of rolling S curves. The sports car screeched through the turns, nearly skidding out several times.

The brothers kept their profiles low, cutting down wind resistance as they rode side-by-side. "Good thing he stuck to the back roads," Frank called to Joe. "If he'd taken the highway, we'd never catch him."

"I guess Ken isn't as smart as he looks," Joe replied. He smiled behind his motorcycle helmet. "There's a trail up ahead that cuts over the switchback. I'm going to take it and try to head him off."

Frank nodded his agreement. When they reached

the middle of the next turn, Joe turned off the street and sped down a dirt trail off the roadside. His bike's tires spun as he hit the loose earth, but Joe leaned left and found firmer ground.

He continued to zoom up the hill. Tall weeds, tangled bushes, and brambles whipped by on either side. At the top of the rise he spotted the sports car rounding the turn below, with Frank close behind.

Joe gunned the throttle and sped downslope. Gravel flew through the air as he skidded down the trail. Twice he had to duck to avoid overhanging branches. He hit the culvert at the roadside and zipped up through the tall weeds and into the roadway once more—right in front of the sports car. For a moment the red car looked like it would hit Joe's motorcycle fully in the side.

Joe accelerated, flew across the road, and dove into the ditch on the far side. The red car swerved to the right, barely missing Joe's rear tire.

The sports car kicked up a huge cloud of dust as it veered from the shoulder back onto the road. It slowed for a moment, then continued on its path.

Joe's wheels slid out from under him, and he nearly tipped over. He fought hard for control, stabbing his right foot down to balance himself. His sneaker hit dirt at the bottom of the culvert, keeping the bike from falling. The impact ran up Joe's leg and rattled his teeth.

Frank pulled into the ditch beside him, skidding almost to a stop. "Are you all right?" the older Hardy called.

"Nothing hurt but my pride," Joe responded. "But don't let him get away!" He pushed out of the ditch and accelerated with Frank at his side.

The sports car had a large lead on them now—and the road was veering from the back country toward the interstate once again.

"If he makes it to the highway, we're cooked," Joe said.

They opened up the throttles, pushing the motorcycles as fast as they'd go. The landscape flattened out ahead and a train track cut directly across the road. The crossing was an old-fashioned one—just a stop sign and two signals next to the shoulder, without the modern no-crossing gate.

As the sports car skidded through the curve near the crossing, the railroad signal lights began to flash and the warning bell sounded. Looking toward their right, the brothers saw a long freight train barreling down the track.

"He wouldn't . . . !" Frank gasped.

The red car didn't slow down as it approached the crossing. The train blared its horn, trying to warn the sports car off. But the car's driver ignored the warning. It flew across the tracks, just ahead of the oncoming train. The car swerved on the far side of the tracks, and its tires kicked up a huge cloud of dust from the shoulder. Then Frank and Joe lost sight of it behind the moving train.

The Hardys skidded to a stop at the crossing and watched helplessly as the train sped past.

"We've lost him!" Joe said.

"Looks like," Frank replied. "Let's not give up yet, though."

Minutes crawled by as the long train chugged over the crossing. Finally the last train car passed and the brothers got a clear view of the road ahead. Frank and Joe looked at each other and smiled.

The red car lay stranded in the culvert on the other side of the tracks.

"I guess racing that train wasn't the best idea after all," Joe said. He and Frank zipped over the tracks and pulled off the road next to the car.

The sports car sat crossways at the edge of the road, its back tires dug into the soft shoulder, its nose pitched down toward the drainage ditch at the bottom of the culvert. It looked really stuck.

The car's convertible top was up, and its tinted windows made it impossible for anyone to see inside. Joe raced to the driver's side door and pulled it open, but found no one in the passenger compartment. Joe frowned. "How could the driver get away?" he asked.

Frank scanned the surrounding terrain. "The weeds in this ditch are pretty high," he said, "and there are some woods at the top of the rise. He could be hiding somewhere nearby. Let's spread out and search. He couldn't have gotten far."

As the brothers started to implement their plan, a thumping sound echoed through the air. "What was that?" Joe asked.

"I think it came from the trunk," Frank said. He walked around behind the Corvette. "The lock has no pull latch. We need a key."

Joe peered into the car's interior. "We're in luck," he said. "The keys are still in the ignition. Catch." He threw the keys to Frank, who promptly opened the trunk.

Inside the tiny, cramped space, lay Ken. He blinked and shielded his eyes from the sun as the trunk opened. "Geez," he said. "I was beginning to think I'd die in here!"

Frank gave him a hand out of the trunk. "How'd you get in the trunk in the first place?" he asked.

"I don't know," Ken replied. "One minute, I was heading for the apartment parking lot, then . . . *wham*! I wake up and I'm on a roller-coaster ride in the dark with my knees pressed up against my chest. Where are we, anyway?"

"On Hebert Boulevard, out near the interstate," Joe said. "Any idea who shanghaied you?"

Ken shook his head. "Like I told you: *wham*!" He rubbed the back of his skull. "Boy, does my head hurt."

"Hop on the back of my bike," Frank said. "I'll take you to the hospital."

"No," Ken said. "No hospitals."

"We'll take you home, then," Joe offered.

"What about my car?"

"It'll have to be towed," Frank said. "The police will probably want to look it over anyway."

"The cops? Why?" Ken asked.

"You were assaulted, locked in the trunk, and kidnapped," Joe said. "Those are all crimes."

"Assuming you're telling us the truth," Frank added.

"Why would I lie about something like this?" Ken asked testily. "You found me in the trunk yourselves."

"We can discuss that with the police," Joe said. "After we take you home."

Ken climbed onto the back of Frank's motorcycle, and the three of them headed back to the band's apartments. When they got there, they found a police cruiser and an ambulance parked in the tree-lined lot. Julie was sitting on a bench nearby, holding an ice pack to her head. Phil, Ms. Greenberg, and the other members of Vette Smash were gathered in a circle around Julie. They all looked grim as the Hardys and Ken pulled up next to them.

"Hey," Ken said, "What's going on? You won't believe what happened to me!"

"You're right," Ray said. "We *won't* believe it."

"We've had enough, Ken," Jackie said angrily. "You're out of the band!"

14 Last Band Standing

"What?" Ken asked, incredulous. "What do you mean I'm out of the band?"

"You tried to run Julie down," Ray said. "We're lucky that she wasn't badly hurt. The police have some questions they want to ask you too."

"Hey!" Ken said angrily. "I got kidnapped and locked in the trunk of my own car. I don't know anything about trying to run Julie down."

"Are you okay, Julie?" Joe asked.

"It's just a little bump on the head," Julie replied. "Nothing to worry about."

"She might have been killed if she hadn't been wearing that motorcycle helmet," Phil said. He glared angrily at Vette Smash's lead guitarist.

"This is nuts!" Ken said. "I didn't do anything."

"Yeah," Jackie said, "funny how you always come out smelling like a rose. Your bungee was cut, but you didn't jump. The lightning generator got Julie but not you, even though you were right next to her. Todd picked up that rigged guitar, not you. And now, somebody else was driving your car and almost ran over Julie."

"That just proves someone is out to get me," Ken said.

"Or somebody was out to get you a lot of publicity," Julie said bitterly. "Maybe you weren't kidding about going solo. It'd be nice to have a ready-made spotlight just waiting for you."

"But I was nearly *killed*," Ken protested.

"Oh, like the rest of us weren't in danger either," Jackie said. "You've pulled us into a lot of crazy schemes. Both the lightning generator and the bungee jump were your idea."

"I think you should all settle down and not do anything rash," Ms. Greenberg said. "I know you're mad at Ken, but breaking up the group now would hurt all of your careers. You've got the big concert at Vince's tonight. Two agents want to sign you right now. But if you back out of that concert or break up the group . . ."

"Yeah," Ken said defiantly. "How are you going to play the gig if I'm not with you? Face it, you need me."

"We could get Kaspar to fill in," Ray said. "He's

played during rehearsals when you were off sulking. He's always willing to help out."

"Geo's good with a guitar," Ms. Greenberg said. "But he can't replace Ken, or Julie, or any of you—either playing or singing. Do you really want a roadie fronting for Vette Smash during the most important concert of your careers?"

The band members looked sullenly at one another, and then at Ken.

"All right," Ray said, "we'll play together tonight—assuming the cops don't haul Ken away. After that, though . . . well, this isn't over."

"You bet it's not," Ken said. "I'm not even sure if I *want* to play with you jerks anymore."

"Please, Ken," Ms. Greenberg said. "For all our sakes. How will it look to Crown and Miyazaki if you walk out now?"

"Yeah, okay," Ken said grudgingly. "We'll play together tonight. After that, though, all bets are off."

The police questioned Ken, but let him go. The paramedics tending to Julie looked Ken over as well. Neither of Vette Smash's guitarists required hospitalization.

As the afternoon stretched toward evening, the band members returned to their own apartments. They decided to postpone that evening's meeting with Ms. Greenberg until the following day. Every member of the group wanted some time to rest.

After saying good-bye, Phil and the Hardys headed home. The three of them cleaned up the motorcycles, then went to the Hardys' house to hang out until the concert.

After dinner Joe checked in with Officer Con Riley, the Hardys' friend at the Bayport Police Department. "Con said the police didn't find any prints on Ken's car—none at all," Joe said. "The whole thing had been wiped clean."

"That's odd," said Frank. "If Ken was behind the wheel, why would he wipe the fingerprints from his own car?"

"Maybe to support his bogus kidnapping story," Phil suggested.

"But when did he have time to wipe the car down?" Frank asked. "He couldn't chance it after getting stuck in the ditch. It would have been tricky enough to stuff himself into the trunk before the train finished crossing the road."

"He could have run away from the scene a lot more easily," Joe admitted. "The police wouldn't have been surprised to find Ken's prints in the car, even if he *had* been kidnapped. Frankly I think the lack of prints tends to support his story."

"So if Ken wasn't driving that car, who was?" Phil asked. "And where did they go after they ditched the car?"

"No way to be sure," Frank said, "but Joe and I stopped looking for the driver after we found Ken.

The real culprit could have been hiding in the woods nearby, or in the tall grass, or in a roadside drain. After we left, it would have been a cinch to wipe down the car, hike up to the highway, and catch a lift away from the scene."

"So we're stuck," Phil said. "There's no way to figure out who tried to run Julie down."

"Like most real-life mysteries, we've got too many suspects rather than too few," Joe said. "Dick Devlin and Green Machine could be looking to put Vette Smash out of business. Crown, Miyazaki, and Greenberg could be trying to build up publicity for the band. . . ."

"Though it's a dangerous way to gain publicity," Phil noted.

"Dangerous, but effective," Joe said. "Vette Smash has been in the news every night this week. Ken, or one of the others, could be trying to pump themselves up before going solo. There are other angles to consider as well. It's just a matter of coming up with a theory that fits all the facts."

"Before anyone else gets hurt," Frank said.

"Or the group breaks up once and for all," Phil added.

The three of them discussed the angles of the case until nearly ten thirty. Then, having reached no conclusions, they piled into the Hardys' van and drove down to Vince's Powerbar for the midnight show.

Phil's backstage pass got them past the hired security and around the crowd of patrons waiting for the performance. Big fireproof curtains had been lowered across the front of the stage, completely shielding the band's setup. More heavy draperies separated the main stage from the dressing rooms and service areas at the back of the club. The stage itself was nearly dark. Everything seemed in place for the performance by the time the three friends arrived.

"Did you notice Dick Devlin out front?" Frank asked as the three of them slipped backstage.

"And Green and a bunch of his bully friends," Phil replied.

"Guess they must have paid their debt to society already," Joe said sarcastically.

"You think security can handle them?" Phil asked.

"After the trouble last night," Frank said, "I'm sure the management will have twice as many guards as they actually need. Nobody wants another riot."

Ken and Jackie stood backstage amid a throng of reporters, giving interviews. They smiled and laughed, and looked altogether different from the grim band members who'd been at one another's throats in the apartment parking lot earlier that day.

"Looks like some serious damage control efforts by the band," Joe said.

"You'd never guess that this morning they were barely talking to one another," Phil said.

Ms. Greenberg lurked in the wings, warily watching the impromptu press conference. When Walker Crown and Kelly Miyazaki arrived, she left her post to schmooze with them.

"I wonder who she's leaning toward?" Frank said.

"With all that's gone on today, I'm amazed she even had a chance to read their proposals," Joe said.

"Where's Julie?" Phil asked. "I saw Ray heading for the refreshment table, but I haven't seen her at all."

"Maybe she's resting in her dressing room," Joe suggested.

Phil nodded. "Probably. Hey, if you guys don't mind, I think I'll check on her."

"Sounds good," Frank replied.

"The band can't play if they're missing one member," Joe said. He paused and looked at Frank.

Slowly the elder Hardy smiled and nodded. "Joe and I will poke around a little more," he said, "to make sure everything's on the up and up."

"We'll start at the buffet," Joe added.

"See you soon, then," Phil said. He took off for the dressing rooms while Frank and Joe headed toward the free food, where they saw Ray.

"Are you ready for the big pyro show?" Ray asked the Hardys. He swallowed a mouthful of potato salad and downed half a can of soda.

Frank and Joe exchanged a questioning glance. "What do you mean?" Frank asked.

"We've got this big flash-and-fire thing going as part of the act tonight," Ray said, "just to show off for the agents. Billie thought they might up their offers if we put on a killer show."

"So, Miyazaki and Crown didn't mind you putting off your decision until tomorrow?" Frank said.

"Nah," Ray replied. "It's not like they're going anywhere."

"Except maybe to Green Machine—assuming things don't work out for Vette Smash," Joe said.

"No way that's going to happen," Ray said. "We're over our spat with Ken. Really. Vette Smash is one big happy family." His practiced smile failed to convince either of the brothers.

"Isn't a pyro display a little risky," Frank asked, "given all the troubles you've had with stunts lately?"

"No sweat," Ray said. "It's already set up, checked, and ready to go. Besides, Ken's too busy to get anywhere near it—so there's no way the 'Fender curse' can strike again." He winked and laughed, then chugged off toward his dressing room.

"Lack of confidence is *not* one of the band's problems," Joe said.

"Yeah, but sabotage is," Frank replied. "Let's take a look at the setup."

"Okay."

The brothers wound their way through the partitioned curtains toward the front of the stage once more. As they walked in the semidarkness, Frank's sneaker scraped across something rough and sandlike. The smell of sulfur wafted into the air. Both Hardys froze.

Frank stooped down, picked up some of the substance between his fingers, and sniffed. "Black powder," he said.

"The explosive they use for pyrotechnics and fireworks displays?" Joe asked.

Frank nodded. "Someone must have spilled it here."

"On purpose, you're thinking," Joe said.

"Yeah, and I think we both know who did it."

"The same person who's sabotaged the other shows," Joe said. "The person with the most to gain if certain members of Vette Smash got hurt. C'mon."

He and Frank dashed through the heavy draperies toward the front of the club. They pushed the final curtain aside and skidded to a stop at the edge of the stage.

On the far side of the platform a lone figure crouched in the darkness, working feverishly on the pyrotechnics display. As the brothers watched, the figure expertly sabotaged one of the powder-filled flash pots.

15 Flash in the Band

"Hold it!" Frank called.

The figure spun toward them, surprised by the brothers' sudden appearance.

Joe's mouth drew into a grim, straight line. "The game's up," he said. "If you know what's good for you, you'll come quietly."

"You guys scared me," the figure said, remaining hidden in the darkness. "What's up?"

"You might as well give up," Frank said. "We're onto you, Kaspar."

Geo Kaspar stepped from the shadows. "Onto me?" he asked. "I'm just doing some final prep on the displays before the concert."

"The pyrotechnic displays next to where Ken and Julie are playing, I'll wager," Frank said. "Sorry,

Kaspar. We know you've been working behind the scenes to sabotage Vette Smash."

"That's crazy," Geo said. "I work for the band. I've been with them for ages."

"Long enough to want a bigger piece of the action," Joe said. "You figured if you could cut out one of the band members—either Julie or, preferably, Ken—you could step in and take their place." He and Frank moved forward slowly, spreading out as they edged toward the saboteur.

"Everybody said you were good on both the musical and technical ends of a guitar," Frank said. "Julie told us that she went to you if she needed her bass fixed. That same expertise allowed you to sabotage the guitar that zapped Grodd Green."

"Of course, you meant to zap Ken," Joe said, smiling grimly. "You turned that mistake around, though, and almost managed to shift blame onto Ken for all the sabotage. Too bad Ken was a klutz with electrical gizmos. He told us that when we first met him. You should have picked a better patsy."

"We've seen you work around the sets though," Frank concluded. "Just like you are now."

Kaspar backed up slowly as the brothers edged toward him. He glanced from one brother to the other, looking for a way out. In his fist he clutched something that looked like a small black pack of cigarettes.

"The saboteur had to be someone with intimate

144

knowledge of Vette Smash's schedule and working habits," Joe said. "Grodd Green and his band didn't have that. Neither did Miyazaki or Crown. Only someone on the inside could have known the band's every move. An insider would also have known the best time to rig the setups without getting caught. Who better to sabotage the band's equipment than a member of Vette Smash's own road crew?"

"You guys are nuts," Kaspar said, snarling. "You're just guessing. You'll never prove any of this."

"Sure we will," Frank said. He and Joe closed in on the big roadie from opposite directions.

"When these pyro displays malfunction, that'll be all the proof we need," Joe said. "We were told the display was checked and ready to go just after we arrived at the theater."

"So," Frank said, finishing his brother's thought, "any trouble with these pyrotechnics is clearly your fault."

"This display isn't going to malfunction," Kaspar said. A smile tugged at the corners of his brutish mouth. "It's going to do exactly what I want it to."

Before the Hardys could react, Kaspar pressed a button on the device in his hand.

A deafening *boom* filled the auditorium, and a dazzling flash of light went off in the brothers' faces.

The Hardys reeled back, blinded. "He's got the

remote control for the pyro display!" Joe said, suddenly realizing what the device in Kaspar's hand was.

"Don't let him get away," Frank said. He blinked back the spots in his eyes, trying to pick out Kaspar from the shadows.

"I'm . . . ugh!" Joe never finished his sentence. Kaspar bashed him on the jaw, causing the younger Hardy to fall backward.

Frank jabbed at one of the blurry images dancing before him. Kaspar stepped out of the way and clouted Frank on the back of the neck with a microphone stand.

Frank stumbled forward, crashing into Joe just as the younger Hardy started to get up. Both of them collapsed in a heap on the floor.

At that, Kaspar laughed. "So long, boys," he said. He pressed another button on his remote control.

Flames shot up from a pot next to Joe and Frank. The brothers rolled out of the way as the fire scorched their hair.

Kaspar backed toward an emergency exit on the far side of the stage. "Give it up, chumps," he said. "You don't stand a chance."

"Split up," Frank said to Joe. "He can't blast us both at once." He stumbled to the right, away from his brother. Joe went left, but tripped over one of the band's guitar stands.

"Oh, yes I can," Kaspar replied. He pressed another button on the control and a fountain of sparks burst up next to Frank. Frank staggered into the curtains at the front of the stage. The heavy fabric wrapped around him, limiting his movement.

"Afraid of a little fire?" Kaspar asked.

Joe crawled blindly through the semidarkness, barely able to see anything. "Keep talking, big mouth," he hissed—but his head crashed into the bass drum.

Kaspar laughed, almost doubling over as he watched the brothers groping blindly around the stage. His eyes must have gotten used to the dark, so he could see. He pressed another button, and more flash pots burst in front of the Hardys.

Joe's fingers found the neck of Julie's guitar. He seized the instrument and whipped it in the direction of Kaspar's mocking laughter.

Kaspar gasped as the solid body of the big bass guitar caught him in the stomach. The air rushed out of his lungs and he fell to his knees. The remote control flew from his hands and smashed onto the stage floor.

Frank rebounded off the curtains and pounced on Kaspar before the big man could recover. Kaspar tried to scratch Frank's face, but Joe dove forward and grabbed the roadie's hands. In less than a minute the brothers wrestled the villain into submission and tied him with his own belt.

The Hardys rose and dusted themselves off.

"Nice throw with that guitar," Frank said, still blinking to clear his vision.

Joe smiled. "I always was good at blind man's bluff!"

By the time Vette Smash hit the stage, the police had already taken Kaspar away. The band rocked Vince's Powerbar like it had never been rocked before, playing three encores and leaving the audience cheering for more. But despite their success, all of the band members—even Ken—decided to turn in early that night. They'd had plenty of excitement for one day.

The next afternoon Vette Smash, Billie Greenberg, the Hardys, and Phil all met for lunch at Kool Kone. The brothers explained the end of the case while the group munched on fried clams, fried scallops, and crab cakes.

"The key turned out to be figuring out who had the most to gain from the trouble," Frank said. "Green Machine topped the list, but they didn't have access to the things necessary to pull the sabotage off—things Geo Kaspar had right at hand."

Joe nodded, popped another scallop into his mouth, and picked up the story. "Kaspar knew Vette Smash's schedule, he could move around backstage freely, he could visit the band members' apartments if he needed to, and he had access to the band's shed—where the bungees, the lightning generator, and the other electronic equipment was kept. It wouldn't take him much time to sabotage the gear, and anyone who would see him messing around would just assume he was working on the setup. His position as an inside man made him nearly unstoppable."

"And very dangerous," Julie added.

"Not even the most reckless promoter would subject his clients to the kind of risks that the saboteur put Vette Smash through," Frank said. "That ruled out Crown, Miyazaki, and Ms. Greenberg as suspects."

"On behalf of the management, I thank you," Ms. Greenberg said, giving a little bow.

Frank laughed. "That left the band itself, and for a while we thought that Ken might be using the trouble as a spectacular kickoff for his own solo career."

"Yeah, thanks," Ken said sarcastically.

"But finding you in the trunk of your own car—a car wiped clean of fingerprints—made that an impossibility," Joe explained.

"Our guess is that Kaspar hoped to put Ken behind the wheel of the car after trying to run Julie down," Frank said. "That's why he stashed Ken in the trunk. He didn't count on Joe and me chasing him. Nor did he count on running off the road during the chase. He was lucky to get away and wipe his prints from the car."

"So, someone was out to get Ken," Joe said, "or

out to get Julie. We realized then that the saboteur had been targeting individual band members, not the band itself. Ken and Julie had lots of trouble, but the sabotage never came close to Jackie or Ray. Why?"

"Maybe Jackie and I were trying to take over the band ourselves," Ray suggested. He laughed menacingly.

Jackie slugged him in the shoulder. "The drummer and the keyboard player trying to oust the lead singers and guitarists. *That* makes sense," she said, smirking.

"We figured that the saboteur didn't want the whole band gone—just part of it," Joe said. "The part he could replace."

"The guitarists!" Phil said.

"Exactly," said Frank. "Putting Ray or Jackie out of business wouldn't have done Kaspar any good. He didn't play drums or keyboards—but he *did* play guitar, pretty well by all accounts."

"So Geo wanted me or Ken out, so he could step in," Julie said.

Joe nodded. "It was simple enough for Kaspar to hand the cut bungee to Ken before the jump, and make it appear to be a random choice."

"And the malfunction of the electrical display was tailor-made for your costume, Julie," Frank added. "All the metal you wore pretty much guaranteed you'd be the lightning's prime target. Ken might've gotten hit too, since you played close together at the front of the stage."

"The front of the stage is where the lighting bar that nearly got Phil killed was positioned," Joe said. "Kaspar scared off the regular technician, then sabotaged the lights, hoping that one of you would get hurt when the display fell."

"But the plan went wrong, and Phil got there before Kaspar could complete the job," Frank explained. "So he pushed Phil over the edge to buy time to escape. If Phil had fallen on Ken or Julie, so much the better."

Ray let out a long, slow sigh. "My mom was right," he said. "She always says problems usually start at home. If we'd fired Geo, we could have solved all our trouble."

"Not all of it," Joe said. "Dick Devlin, Grodd Green, and the Green Machine fans did their share too. They made the threatening call to the band's answering machine the day before the bungee jump, hoping Vette Smash might chicken out. They also called the radio station and suggested that people storm the band's apartment to demand their money back from the canceled concert. And, of course, Green and his thugs started the brawl in the underground parking garage."

"They were playing right into Geo Kaspar's hands," Frank said, "even though Kaspar didn't arrange for it to happen."

"So, did Green Machine poison Geo, or did he poison himself?" Ken asked.

"Neither," Frank replied. "When we discovered the empty poison bottle, Kaspar had to think fast. He faked his own illness to divert suspicion from himself and to get away from the scene of the crime."

"Faking being poisoned also gave him time to lurk around backstage and set up his next bit of sabotage," Joe said. "The booby-trapped guitar."

"Boy," Jackie said, "if Geo wanted to be in a band so badly, he should have started his own group."

"And work his way up from the bottom?" Joe said. "Not a chance."

"So," Ms. Greenberg said between bites of fried clam, "Geo figured with Ken or Julie out of the band, he'd be the only chance to keep Vette Smash going. The choice would be to either let him play, or start all over again."

"Okay," Phil said, "I get all that. But who was it that Frank overheard plotting in the alley behind the Browning?"

"That was me," Ms. Greenberg said sheepishly. "I was trying to convince Walker Crown to sign us up. He was cautious, though, and wanted to see what Green Machine had to offer."

"Our police contacts confirmed that it was Crown who followed the band in that gray rental car," Joe said. "He spent a lot of time skulking around, trying to find out more about the talent—their habits and such. I checked Walker's business records. He signed a couple of acts that didn't work out last year. It hurt his business. He didn't want to make that kind of mistake again."

"Miyazaki seemed like the more cautious agent," Frank said, "but behind his boisterous attitude, Walker Crown was being very careful."

"So," Phil said, "which one of them is the band going to sign with?"

The members of Vette Smash looked quizzically at one another and then laughed. "To tell you the truth," Ms. Greenberg said, "we've barely had time to think about it."

"Either way," Frank said, "you've definitely got a head start on publicity."

"Too bad Geo got greedy," Ray said. "We'd have taken care of him."

"But he would have been a roadie," Frank said, "and he wanted a lot more. If his plan had worked, he'd have ridden Vette Smash's star all the way to the top."

"Now we get to ride that star ourselves," Julie said, "thanks to you two, and Phil."

"Kaspar was looking for a trip to the big time," Joe said, "but instead, all he got was a trip to the big house!"

Frank smiled. "Right—and he'll be singing the 'Bayport County Prison Blues' for a very long time."